REVENGE IN KIND

A Novella

REVENGE IN KIND

A Novella

K.C. Bailey

K.C. BAILEY

ISBN 978-0-9644935-3-7

Meerkat Publications
www.meerkatpublications.org

For Pono and Miki

TABLE OF CONTENTS

ONE

One's natural tendencies, the quirks of personality that dictate how we perform tasks at hand, help define which jobs we enjoy. Maria De La Cruz was a tidy person who was satisfied only when everything was clean and uncluttered. For her, every item had its place and she derived fair pleasure in keeping things kempt. This trait served her well in her job as accounting clerk for the auto dealership where she worked. And, if she had been able to fulfill her life, it would have made her the exceptional nurse that she aspired to become. But that was not to be.

It was a Tuesday afternoon and Maria had just finished clearing her desk and had clocked out. She pulled her thick black hair into a ponytail and checked her watch, which read 4:59 PM. She was exactly on time.

She donned a headset to listen to an English-language tape, grabbed her purse, and walked swiftly between new cars in the showroom. She smiled and waved at her co-worker, a young salesman named Romeo Lombardi. In her heavily accented English she called to him, "Have a good night, Romeo!"

He grinned and replied, "Hey, how about a movie after work on Friday?" But she didn't hear him and exited onto the street.

Traffic was already heavy as she waited to cross the intersection. She was softly repeating English phrases from her instruction tape. The light changed and she walked swiftly to the bus stop and stood to wait in a line that was forming along the curbside. She was lost in her language lesson as a dented, rusting, blue Camaro slowed to a stop in front of her.

George Lehman, the driver, was of slim build and a had thin, pock-marked face. His eyes were deep-set with dark circles under them, and his head was shaved, adding to his cadaver-like appearance. No doubt, going through early life being so unattractive would promote having a chip on his shoulder. But what most people reacted to was his demeanor; he had an air of malice about him that made people move out of his way despite his small stature.

Lehman rolled down the passenger side window and leaned over. "Hey, Sweetie, you want a ride?"

Maria looked up and saw him. Recognition and fear filled her eyes. She shook her head and involuntarily stumbled a few steps backward, trying to put others between herself and Lehman. She ripped off her headset and turned her back to the street, crossing herself with tightly closed eyes.

The bus arrived and honked at Lehman. He laughed with a sound that was more like a dry cough, pointed a finger at her and lowered his thumb in a mocking "gunshot." He pulled away from the curb, calling out, "See ya later, Sweetie!"

Maria was shaking. The crowd entering the bus jostled her and she was swept along with everyone boarding the bus. She took a seat next to a window as the bus pulled away and entered traffic.

For several blocks, Maria stared out the window with tears in her eyes. Then the bus stopped right in front of a gun shop. Maria focused on it. She scrambled up and, pushing her way through the crowd standing in the aisle, exited.

She stood indecisively outside the shop. Then she turned away and stood at the bus stop again. Her eyes were closed as she recalled to herself how the man in the blue car had come only occasionally to the bus stop at first, but now he showed up frequently. She had even seen him follow her at a distance when she walked from the bus stop to her duplex. No, she thought to herself, he was not going to stop. And she knew he was somehow becoming bolder. She was certain in her own mind that he intended to hurt her, but she didn't know what to do about it. She had to do something to save herself. She shivered, crossed herself, and strode with determination into the shop.

Inside, it took a few moments for her eyes to adjust to the darkness of the store compared to the brilliant sunlight outside. She didn't see anyone. "Hello?" she called.

"Back here," a voice replied.

She walked to the back where a tall, bony clerk stood behind a glass counter filled with pistols. He was chewing gum and reading a magazine. Behind him was a wide rack filled with rifles. "What kin I do ya fer?" he asked. He removed his reading glasses, the joints of which were held together with tape.

She felt unsure about what he had said. She softly spoke. "I need to buy a gun please."

"What kine-a gun ya lookin' fer?"

Again, she couldn't understand him. She plunged on, "I need to buy a gun please. Can you help me?

"Well, what'cha gonna do wit it?"

This time she got it. She explained, "I am afraid. A man follows me. Maybe if I have a gun, he cannot hurt me."

"Lady, even if I could sell ya a gun, ya couldn't legally carry it around w'it ya without carry permit. And I cain't sell it to ya if I don' do a backgrounder. Takes three days to hear back, then I can sell. And ya gotta have a valid ID."

"I no carry it around with me. I will keep it only in my house."

"Even so, I cain't sell one t'ya without a backgrounder. D'ya got a driver's license?

"No, no license."

"Ya gotta be a citizen or a legal resident. You a citizen?"

The confidence she'd felt upon making her decision to buy a gun was melting. "No, I am not a citizen yet."

Maria set her headset and purse on the counter. She was trying to form the words in her mind that might convince him. If she were at home in Mexico, she would know exactly how to handle the situation, but here everything was different. There were rules about everything and making a reasonable case, coupled with a bit of money to grease the process, didn't work here.

"Please, mister, I need a gun. This man. This man. I know he wants to hurt me. He follows me. He is everyday."

"Sorry. No can do. Rules are da rules. I suggest ya go to da cops."

She gathered her things, turned away with fresh tears in her eyes, and slowly walked outside into the bright heat of the afternoon.

It was dusk when she disembarked at the bus stop near her home. She walked down her street in the quiet, run-down neighborhood of small frame houses. Its most attractive feature was the curb-side row of large old trees, whose roots buckled the sidewalks treacherously.

Maria approached her duplex, head down. She looked up and saw the Camaro parked down the street under a tree. She gasped and looked around to see if Lehman was nearby. Not seeing him, she hurried up the sidewalk to her door. She was thinking that he might be hidden nearby, waiting to jump out and grab her. As her fear mounted, she fumbled her keys and dropped them in her urgency to get inside. Panic overtook her as finally she got the door open and lurched inside, spilling her purse and headset onto the floor. She slammed the door, locked it, and leaned her back against it, sobbing.

Across the street, Lehman stepped from behind a tree. He smiled, lit a cigarette, then walked to the Camaro. Humming tunelessly, he got in and drove away.

Slowly Maria regained her composure. I have to think clearly of what to do, she told herself. She went from room to room, trying to secure the house. She made sure all windows were locked and shades pulled. She jammed a kitchen chair under the back door handle and moved a heavy chair against the front door. She took a knife from the kitchen drawer and placed it next to the rosary on the table by her bed. She then knelt before the small cross on her wall and prayed.

When satisfied that she had done all she could do, she went to remove her makeup and wash her face. While at the sink, she heard the slam of a car door outside. She jumped, dropped the soap and rushed to her bedroom. In a panic, she dragged a small chest of drawers in front of the bedroom door. Looking around, not knowing what else she could do, she grasped the rosary from the bedside table, curled into a fetal position on the bed and wept. The bedside clock showed it was only eight PM.

***

Several miles away, Lehman left a hamburger joint, got into his Camaro, and headed home. There was a light drizzle, and his windshield wipers smeared the rain, making streetlights a streaky blur.

Lehman rocked back and forth as he drove and whispered to himself, "Tonight. Yeah. Tonight. Tonight."

The rain was heavier as Lehman pulled into a driveway of a dark, deserted house. Tall weeds were overtaking hulks of discarded refrigerators, washers, and dryers that littered the yard and eerily flashed white in his headlights. The long drive curved around to the back of the house and ended at a two-story garage.

Lehman, humming tunelessly, climbed the exterior stairs to his apartment over the garage. Inside, he flipped on a single-bulb overhead light. The room contained only minimal furniture. Although it was his home, it did not look lived in.

He went to his dresser and put on a pair of latex gloves. He then gathered a second pair of latex gloves, a condom packet, flashlight, a knife, and a roll of duct tape. He carefully wiped them down and packed them into his black fanny pack. He laid the pack in the center of the dresser and stared at it. Slowly, what passed for a smile worked the corners of his mouth upward.

Lehman removed the gloves. He then striped, carefully folding each item of clothing as he went. Naked, he went into his bathroom and shaved his already hairless body.

After showering, he dressed in clean black clothing, turned off the light, and sat in the dark, smoking.

He viewed this quiet time before going out as preparation. It wasn't that he needed to review what he would do or how. Rather, he increased his anticipation for what was to come by thinking about their eyes, their whimpers and pleading. They were all alike, self-important little beauty queens who looked down on him. He looked forward to their fear and to overpowering them.

At one AM, Lehman left his apartment and drove to Maria's duplex. As he approached, he turned his headlights off. He sat in his car a few moments, relishing the rush that he always got just before he had what he called "an event." Then he donned his latex gloves and got out of the Camaro, closing the door as softly as he could. It was a moonless night, just as he'd planned, but there was still the streetlight, so he kept to the shadows. He made his way soundlessly to the back of the duplex.

Inside, Maria was in a fitful sleep. The cross had fallen from her hand. Sweat beaded on her brow, glistening in the yellow streetlight that edged in around the window shades.

At the back door, Lehman cut open the screen door to reach in and unlock it. Then he used a rock to break a window pane in the door.

At the sound of shattering glass, Maria awoke with a start. There was silence. She listened intently, not sure whether she'd heard something or dreamed it. Her heart was pounding so loudly that she felt she couldn't hear clearly.

Lehman reached his hand through the broken pane and released the door chain and the deadbolt. He shone his flashlight through. He dislodged the chair from under the door handle and it clattered to the floor.

Now she was sure that he was coming for her. Maria was at first frozen by her terror, then she bolted out of bed, searching for the knife. In her haste, she dropped it and it scooted away. She was fumbling, shaking uncontrollably. She looked at the window, then the closet, evaluating which to try. She ran to the window and pushed aside the shade and tried to lift the window. The roller shade clattered upward, filling the room with streetlight. The window was jammed. She scrambled across the room to the closet, shut herself in, and cowered behind the hanging clothes.

In the kitchen, Lehman stood quietly listening to the shuffling noises coming from the bedroom. When it was totally quiet, he crossed the kitchen and walked slowly down the hallway to the bedroom door. He turned off his flashlight and listened. He could hear nothing. He tried the bedroom door but found it locked. He kicked it in, knocking over the small chest she had placed in front of it.

Lehman stepped into the room, making sure she was not behind the door. He stood still in the center of the room, listening. Gently he said, "Sweetie, I'm here."

There was no sound. "Where are you? Are you hiding? I like that. I love hide-and-seek." Then, in a singsong voice, he called, "Come out, come out, wherever you are."

Inside the closet, Maria could hear him clearly. Involuntarily she made a low moan of terror.

Lehman looked at the closet and smiled. He began to slowly strip, carefully folding and stacking his clothes on the dresser top. From his fanny pack, he took out the tape, cut a strip, and tagged it to the edge of the dresser. Then he took out the condom packet and placed it on the bedside table. He closed his eyes with the intense rush he felt.

"Yes, you're waiting for me. I know where you are. Come out now and I won't hurt you." His tone was soft, almost kind. He was very relaxed, but also excited.

Lehman walked to the closet, jerked open the door, and smiled. Trembling uncontrollably, Maria shrank backward. As he reached in to grab her, she screeched. He angrily jerked her out by the hair. Viciously, he yelled, "Shut up!"

Her knees gave way as she urinated on the floor. Maria moaned loudly.

He grabbed her by the neck and pulled her up. "Stand up and be still and you'll live!"

He yanked her head backward, tightening his grip in her hair. He put his face close to hers and hissed, "Put your hands behind your back, palm-to-palm."

Maria stood rigidly, unable to speak or move.

"Now!"

She obeyed. He let go of her and wrapped the strip of duct tape in a figure 8 around her wrists. He then put a piece over her mouth.

"Lie down!"

He threw her onto the bed. She bolted off the other side and tried to ram her body through the window. He ran around the bed, grabbed her and raised his hand.

In a well-aimed slam of the base of his palm, he broke her nose, stunning her. He threw her onto the bed and ripped her clothing off. Blood poured from her nose and she choked, struggling for air.

Lehman carefully opened his condom package.

***

Some men are blessed with having a presence, a self-confidence that sways others to believe in and follow them. Combine that with good looks and a pleasing personality and you have a popular man. Such was Chris Coxon, a 40-year-old detective with the Austin Police Department. He was not particularly tall, just under six feet, but he *seemed* tall. His hair was dark and curly, cut close to his head, and was beginning to grey slightly at the temples. His nose was slightly aquiline, his jaw square, with a small dimple in his chin. To top it all off, he was in extremely good physical shape.

Inside Maria De La Cruz's bedroom there were several forensic technicians, two uniformed officers, Detective Coxon, and his partner. Oddly, Coxon was the one who looked out-of-place. Dressed in a crisp shirt, jacket, and tie, he looked more like he belonged in a company boardroom than at a crime scene.

Standing next to him was his partner, Detective Seng Kang. The two were a study in physical contrasts. Kang was an Oriental who was dressed in a florid shirt, jeans, and jogging shoes. He was so tall that he made Coxon seem short. Whereas Coxon conveyed an air of all-business, Kang was the opposite. He was ever-relaxed and seemingly always on the edge of a laugh.

The two detectives were looking down at De La Cruz's body. Coxon said, "Tape over the mouth again. I guess when we turn her we'll see figure eight tape around the wrists."

Kang gestured toward the knife protruding from her chest, "Well, the knife is a new twist."

Coxon glanced at his partner to see if it was supposed to be humor. He grimaced at the sight of Kang's shirt. "Every time I look at you today, my eyes hurt. So, where do you get those awful shirts? Can't you wear normal clothes?"

"Told you last time you asked. An Aloha shirt. You know, what guys wear on the Honolulu force. Symbol of how relaxed and friendly we are."

"Yeah, well, you're in Austin now, not Honolulu anymore. You should do as the Romans, you know. Why'd you ever leave Hawai'i in the first place? You must be crazy, but ... yeah, you're crazy alright."

"Came here so I could work with you, Chris. Wanted to be with the best."

Coxon turned to look at Kang to see if he's being sarcastic. Kang smiled pleasantly.

Kang continued, "Besides, didn't get crime like this in Honolulu. People there aren't whacked out like the guy that did this."

"You wanted to come here so you could see this shit?"

"Of course not. Just want to catch the pervert that did it."

Coxon turned to a uniformed cop standing nearby. "Do we know if the knife is hers?"

"It matches the ones in her kitchen, so probably."

Coxon murmured softly to himself, "So he didn't bring it with him." Then, more loudly, he asked the cop, "Where's the guy that called it in?"

"He's out back. Name's Romeo. Romeo Lombardi."

Kang laughed. "Name like that, has to be a suspect, right?"

Coxon, whose wit was dry, often didn't share Kang's lighthearted approach. He replied seriously, "Whoever did this wouldn't call it in. But maybe he knows something he doesn't know he knows." Then, again addressing the uniformed cop, asked, "What's he driving?"

"A green KIA."

Coxon turned to Kang, "Let's get Summerfeld to organize the neighborhood canvas. Make sure that the questions include whether anyone has noticed a car parked in front here recently. If they have, see if they can describe it."

"Want to ask if they've seen a green Kia?"

"We don't want it to be like the Washington sniper case. Remember? Right after each shooting, cops asked whether anyone had seen a white van with a broken taillight. Of course, everyone said they had. It turned out that the shooters were in a car, not a van, it wasn't even white, and there was no broken taillight."

A forensic technician spoke, "Detective Coxon, we're finished. We can turn her now."

A technician stepped forward and turned Maria. They saw the tape in figure eight around her wrists. Coxon and Kang exchanged a look. The crucifix fell to the floor. Coxon picked it up with his gloved hand and sadly shook his head.

Kang said, "Hope it helped her."

Coxon replied, "Obviously it didn't."

Kang added, "I mean helped her get to heaven."

They left the room as technicians began to bag the body and sheets. Outside, they approached Lombardi, who was sitting in a lawn chair in the shade of a tree. Coxon turned a chair backward, sat down across from Lombardi, and rested his forearms on the chair back. He peered at Lombardi, looking for nervousness. But Lombardi was relaxed.

"Mr. Lombardi, I'm Detective Coxon and this is Detective Kang. We'd like to ask you some questions." He obtained some basic information then asked, "So how come you came over here to her house?"

"She was always punctual getting to work. Could set your clock by her. When she didn't show up today, I got worried. Boss called her, but she didn't answer her phone. I decided to drive by on my lunch break and see if everything was okay. When she didn't answer the door, I walked around here and saw..." Lombardi's voice trailed off and he gestured toward broken door.

"Did you enter?"

"No."

"So, what then?"

"Used my cell to call 911. They told me to stay here, so I did."

"What do you know about her?"

"Not much. Came from Mexico. Planned to go to nursing school as soon as her English was better. My boss would know more about her than me."

"Yeah, well, we'll check all that out. But first I want to hear from you. Have you ever been inside her house?"

"Never."

Kang asked, "So we won't find your prints in there, right?"

"No, Sir. I didn't even touch the door. I sat in this chair right here and my prints are on it, but that's all."

"When was the last time you saw Ms. De La Cruz?"

"When she said goodnight to me when she left work yesterday. She left at 5:00 sharp. She has to because she catches a bus nearby at five-twelve."

Coxon and Kang exchanged a look. Kang nodded.

Coxon realized that there was not much more that Lombardi could contribute. He stood. Kang took the cue and handed Lombardi a pad and pen as Coxon said, "Give us your address and contact information. Write clearly."

Coxon and Kang walked out of Lombardi's earshot. Kang said, "I can get a canvas at the bus stop. Maybe someone saw if she got on the bus yesterday or if she got another ride. But I need a photo."

"Okay. I'll get Garcia to make the call to the family in Mexico. No photos of her inside. We'll have to look harder for her passport, or maybe the family can send us some shots of her."

Coxon looked at his watch, then said, "Yeah, well I've got to get over to the community college. I have an outreach talk to give there in thirty-five minutes."

"Still trying to communicate with the little heathens, huh? They'll never listen. Come on, I will get you there on time."

"Just get me there alive."

***

Teenagers can excel at conveying insolence, boredom, and ennui all at the same time. Coxon stood in front of 25 college freshmen and he sensed it. He wasn't reaching them; he was spinning his wheels. They were slouching, not making eye contact with him, and in some cases checking their cells in their laps. He paused and thought to himself that rather than wasting time here, he ought to be back at the office working on catching Maria De La Cruz's killer.

Coxon continued, "Murder here in Austin is down by 12.9% over last year. Robbery is down 6.7%. Rape is the crime that's growing — up by 10.5%." Even to himself, Coxon sounded like a bore. "One reason for the increase is directly due to date rape drugs."

Some of the male students sniggered. Coxon felt his irritation rising. He fought it back and plunged on. "We have had many more women this year raped under the influence of GHB, Rohypnol, and Ketamine. Rohypnol is particularly heavily used here in Austin because it's legal in Mexico. It's just too easy to bring it across the border."

There was more sniggering. Coxon paused and looked at one male who was grinning and rolling his eyes. Coxon felt the heat of anger swelling. He walked over and looked down, "What's funny about that? Explain it to me."

The student said nothing, but kept grinning. Coxon stared at him until the grin disappeared and the student began to squirm.

Behind the guy, a female reached across the aisle to hand a note to another girl. Coxon reached out and intercepted it. As he walked back to the front of the room, he looked down at the note, which read: "This guy is really hot!" He stuck it in his pocket and acted like nothing had happened.

Coxon turned and stood looking at the students for several uncomfortable moments. At least he now had their attention. He decided to try again.

"How many of you would agree that a man who needs to drug a woman to kiss her ... to have sex with her ... is not really much of a man at all?"

The students were silent and Coxon waited. Gradually, female students began to raise their hands. Then males began to raise theirs. The grinner was the last to raise his.

"Okay, good."

The students lowered their hands. They were attentive, expectant. Coxon didn't want to lose them. He needed to get one or more of them to say something.

"So what do you think is wrong with a guy who uses drugs on women in order to rape them?" He waited. Gradually they realized that he was not going to answer his own question.

A student raised her hand. Coxon pointed at her and nodded.

"I think he's an inept prick."

Coxon smiled, "Well, I guess that pretty well sums it up."

Some students laughed. Some body language began to improve; the females were no longer slouching.

Another female added, "And he has low self-esteem."

A male chimed in, "He doesn't make it in sports." Coxon thought to himself that the comment didn't compute, but he said nothing. It was better to have them talking than not.

The first female student said, "Yeah, well, we know these guys exist. So, what do we do about them?"

Coxon was relaxing more, his anger gone. "Excellent question. That's why we need to talk. To make sure date rape doesn't happen to you ... and, guys, don't think this message is just for women. Males have also been drugged and then either beaten or raped."

Coxon waited while murmuring among males died down, then continued. "My advice boils down to one rule: control what you consume."

A girl with so many piercings that it almost made Coxon wince spoke up, "Yeah, I've heard that. But, like, that's saying to your date, 'Excuse me, but I don't trust you. I think you're likely to rape me, so I'll go to the bar and get my own drink'."

The grinner said, "Yeah. I don't think I'd ask a girl out again if she did that to me."

Coxon said, "Those attitudes are what the date rape offenders depend on. What we need to do here is change our culture to match the times. How can we do that?"

The students remained silent, all eyes on Coxon for the answer.

"Come on, guys, what could you do to make your date comfortable about drinking a drink, for example?"

A burly guy who looked like he must be a football played spoke, "Say to her, 'Darling, would you go to the bar and get us a couple of drinks?' And I'd let her pay for them too!"

The students laughed a little too much. Coxon had the sense that they would laugh at anything this guy wanted them to. There was an air of deference to him in the way that they turned to look at him when he spoke. Coxon decided to use him as the principal player when he started the role-playing exercise.

Another male said, "Ask her to come to the bar with you and carry the drinks back." The student who'd just spoken looked at the burly student to see his response. The big guy smiled and nodded, which brought more laughter.

The same student spoke again, "Or maybe tell her to go get her own damned drink!"

Coxon didn't like the direction the discussion was going, but decided to let it run for a bit more before intervening.

The grinner joined in, "Ask her if she's afraid of date rape before you go out. If she is, don't take her out."

One of the females turned on him. "Some of us take this seriously. This is a real problem, even if *you* don't get it." Then she turned back to Coxon, saying, "But, like, you know, it really is awkward."

"So, what can you do?" Coxon asked.

Three of the women spoke almost simultaneously. "We could go to the bar with our date."

"We could try to go only to restaurants or bars where waiters serve the drinks."

"On double dates, we could go to the bathroom one-at-a-time so that the other girl could watch the drinks."

The burly guy spoke again, "The bathroom one-at-a-time? Now that would be a culture change!"

There was more laughter and Coxon sensed the timing was right to change the direction of the lecture. He pointed at the big guy and motioned to him. He knew he had to get everyone involved and using this guy would do the trick. "Let's do some role-playing here. Come on up here."

The big guy grinned, heaved his hulk out of the desk, put his cell phone away and came forward. The students stirred, interested.

***

Sometimes spending time doing something totally different from daily routine recharges one's mental batteries almost like a nap. That was the way Coxon felt as he got off the elevator to go to his office after his outreach lecture. The role-playing had gone well and he met his objective. Young people often thought themselves invincible and he had convinced them to take care, that indeed they could be targets of evil. He had raised their consciousness of the problem.

As he strode down the hallway, Coxon encountered Detective Raul Garcia, a heavy-set no-nonsense man whose demeanor bespoke a certain tiredness with the world. Garcia asked in a disinterested way, "How did it go at the school?"

Coxon replied, "Thick."

"Huh?"

"With people that age, the hormones in the air are so thick you could cut them with a knife."

Garcia was sure that he was not interested in pursuing that conversation. "Oh ... Say, I finally reached De La Cruz's father. It's pretty tough getting anything out of him. He can't quit crying. Anyway, she has no relatives here. She came to Austin because of the schools. The language school helped her get the student visa. Summerfeld is going over there in the morning. They have her passport as well as some school photos. Then we'll do the bus stop canvas."

"Great. Thanks."

Garcia proceeded down the hall as Coxon entered his own office and almost bumped into Cecilia Drake, the Department's public affairs representative. She was a short, stout woman who had a hurried air about her as if she were always late. But was also ever-cheerful. She waved a sheaf of papers. "Oh, hi, Chris! I need you to look at a copy of the draft press release on De La Cruz. I'm under a lot of pressure to get it out."

"Yeah, right. Everyone wants to know if this is a serial killer case."

She handed it to him. She fidgeted while he read. As he finished, she asked, "Add anything? Subtract?"

"Let's take out the part about the perpetrator using duct tape. Right now, other than rape, that is the only common thread between these killings. Also, the part about her dying due to a stab wound may not be accurate. Take it out. My bet is that the autopsy will show she died of asphyxiation. We'll know tomorrow or as soon as they can get to her."

Drake thanked him and swooshed out of the office. Coxon sat his desk for another hour going though the files of the three women who had been raped and murdered in the past few months. He felt certain that it was indeed a serial killer at work.

It was 5:30 PM when Kang stuck his head in the doorway. Coxon was rubbing his eyes tiredly. "Hey, Seng. Any news?"

"Unfortunately, no. Listen, I'm headed out. Just wanted to stop by, let you know that De La Cruz's boss had nothing useful to add."

Coxon shook his head. "God, I have such a really bad feeling about this. This is the third rape-murder that appears to be by the same guy. We haven't got even one lead."

Kang got the signal that his partner needed to talk to him. He stepped into the office and sat on edge of desk.

"We rely way too much on forensics and the telltales the perps leave behind. It's almost like if we don't have DNA, you know, we don't have a case.

"Yeah, and this guy doesn't seem to make those mistakes. Unbelievable. No prints. Not a single hair, no semen, no blood. Nothing seems to tie together either."

Coxon stood and walked to the map on the wall and tapped locations. "Tate on the east side, Kipplinger on the north. Now De La Cruz over here."

Kang nodded, "Yeah. And, Tate was a grade-school teacher; Kipplinger was an insurance secretary. De La Cruz, an accounting clerk."

"They had very different physiques and hair coloring. Where's the theme, Kang?"

"Wish I knew." Kang looked at his watch. "Well, we'll start anew tomorrow and try to figure out what to do next. Sorry to bolt. Gotta get to the airport. June's coming back from her shoot in Chicago tonight. Hey, wanna come to dinner with us Friday night?"

"No, thanks. I've got two sculptures I have to finish, both promised for that big exhibit coming up."

Kang stood. "Okay. You're gonna miss some great chow. She's making Hmong food, a couple of dishes my mother taught her."

Coxon grinned, "I still don't know why you don't just call it Chinese. It's so much easier to pronounce and that's what it really is."

Kang laughed. This was a conversation he and his partner had in many forms, almost a little ritual that was a thread in the fabric of their relationship. Each knew exactly what the other would say. They could probably even reverse roles and get the dialog right.

"Your ignorance is showing again, Coxon. We Hmong are not Chinese, although our ancestors came from an area that is now in China. I keep telling you my family came from Laos, not China."

"Yeah, Yeah. Well, you look Chinese to me and your food tastes Chinese."

Kang, still smiling, said "You are so politically incorrect. You should be sent to sensitivity training. I really ought to complain about you to HR."

"And if you do, I will turn you in for sexually harassing me!"

The joking had run its course, so Coxon asked, "So what was June doing in Chicago?"

"She was modeling ads for a new line of perfume. Oh, and I didn't tell you. She's going to be on the cover of *Vanity Fair* next month!"

"Wow! You know, you never explained to me how you could catch a woman like that—beautiful, graceful, talented, rich. What does she see in a guy like you, a guy that can't even dress right?"

This was also one of Kang's favorite banters with Coxon. "Easy to explain. I'm a delightful partner..."

Coxon cut him off, saying, "I hadn't noticed that."

Kang ignored the interruption. "...in life. June and I have a relationship, something you don't know anything about, Coxon."

In the ritual, this is when Coxon would act affronted. "I have a lot of relationships."

"That's what I mean. You don't get to know any one woman well. You just go out with escorts or one-night-stands you pick up at art shows. Sometimes I think that's really why you're an artist. It's a tool to pick up women!"

"Hey, don't be judgmental. There's nothing wrong with going out with lovely women who spend the night with me."

"No, man, I'm not criticizing. Just explaining why you don't have a beautiful, smart, fantastic woman like June on your arm. You avoid having a relationship."

"Yeah, well, I know where a relationship leads— demands, demands. I don't want kids, I don't want make-up all over my bathroom, and I don't want to argue about money. In my kind of relationships, I don't have any of that crap. And, enough of this, I'm heading for the gym."

Coxon knew that this is where he had to end the conversation, or he'd have to endure Kang's retort that he had none of these issues with June.

Kang grinned and started for the door, vowing aloud that they'd finish this conversation another time.

***

Coxon loosened his tie, picked up his jacket, and headed for the basement gym, as he did every Sunday, Tuesday, and Thursday, and sometimes in between. This was one of his favorite ways to end the day. In a way, he didn't look forward to the exercise at all and would rather just go home. On the other hand, he wanted to have that delicious feeling when he was done. It would be a mixture of tired muscles, calmness, and a sense of accomplishment. It would be almost euphoria.

He changed clothes in the locker room and went to the corner of the gym to start with a few stretches and yoga moves. During this warm-up, he reflected on his conversation with Kang about women. He mused that Kang was actually wrong about the pick-ups at art shows. Although it had happened a few times, he had learned the hard way how such liaisons could turn ugly when a husband found out. So, he had pretty much stuck to women from an upscale escort service, but that had its downsides too. For example, he couldn't remember the last time he'd kissed a woman on the lips. He couldn't bear the thought of where the escorts' lips had been perhaps only an hour before. Likewise, even though he'd had a vasectomy, he always wore a condom during copulation to protect himself against sexually transmitted diseases. Increasingly, his method of choice was fellatio followed by a shower.

He moved across the gym to spend 20 minutes on the treadmill. Thinking about sex led him to think of a question that had always baffled him: how could a man enjoy rape? He wondered whether he could even reach orgasm if he knew the woman was distressed. Hell, he sometimes found it difficult to have sex if he sensed boredom from his partner.

He thought that a prerequisite to physical assault of a woman must begin with dehumanizing her. Actually, that was a precursor to all kinds of horrors. In the case of any pogrom, the ringleaders would begin by denigrating the victims, painting them as infidels, criminals, or predators. But how did a man, or a group of men, reach a conclusion that women as a gender are somehow less than human and therefore reasonable prey? Try as he might, Coxon could not wrap his mind around the concept.

At 6:30 PM, it was time to meet the Department's weight trainer, which was the best part of the routine on Tuesdays and Thursdays. He loved working with weights and increasing his awareness of individual muscles in his body.

The weight training session lasted only 20 minutes, but by the end of it, Coxon's muscles were screaming and he was sweating profusely. The trainer was spotting him on presses and told him that he thought that was enough for the day. But he always said that at the 20-minute mark, as if it were the effort expended rather than the time passed.

Coxon stood and thanked him, then wrapped a towel around his neck. He would spend some time cooling down before showering and heading home. Usually, he'd sit on one of the machines and mindlessly watch the news, but tonight he saw the lights on in the next room, the mirrored room where yoga and karate classes were taught. He strolled slowly toward the doorway to see what was going on in there. What he saw was pretty interesting, so he leaned against the doorjamb, watching.

A woman whom he'd never seen before was practicing karate with the department instructor. She was a black belt and it showed. She was remarkably lithe, fast, and effective. He thought to himself that he'd never seen anyone as good as she, including the instructor. As he watched intently, the weight trainer came and looked over Coxon's shoulder.

Coxon told him, "I sure wouldn't want to be on the receiving end of her kick. But, god, she's so graceful, so powerful. I've never seen her here before. Who is she?"

The trainer smiled, adding "And beautiful! Yeah, Chris, that's what everyone thinks. Get in line! She's new to the Department and I hear she's untouchable in more ways than one."

***

25

Meanwhile, Kang and June arrived at their apartment. He brought her suitcase inside and closed the door. She wrapped her arms around his neck and held him close. He spoke softly into her hair, telling her how much he'd missed her. She kissed him and while they were embracing, her stomach growled loudly. They both laughed. "I guess one of us is pretty hungry because she wouldn't eat airline food, right?"

"I am a little peckish," she said.

"Does that mean 'hungry' for the rest of us dolts? So how about cheese and wine?"

Without waiting for an answer, he went to the kitchen and started making two plates of cheese and crackers. She opened a bottle of Chianti, sampled it, then poured two glasses and carried them to the living room coffee table. He brought in the plates and they settled on the couch.

June asked how his work was going. He told her about the De La Cruz case and how frustrating it was to have no solid clues.

"The part I like about this job is when we get the bad guy. The part I despise is the waiting and apprehension about whether we will get the bad guy. This case has me worried."

"Seems to me like you always get the bad ones. Sometimes it just takes a while."

"Yeah, and during that 'while' more crimes can be committed. June, anybody else who gets raped and killed is kind of like my fault. If I catch him in time, no one else goes down. If I don't, every other victim is because I couldn't do my job fast enough."

"You're awfully hard on yourself, as if you're the only one responsible. Does Chris do this to himself too?"

"He's worse, probably because he has no real life other than the Department and his sculpting." He reflected a moment. "You know, it's funny, I guess one helps the other. I mean, when his work is really tough, his art is better, more prolific. And when he's really into the art, it seems to clear his mind for work."

"Just art and work? Has he ever been married?"

Kang laughed at the thought. "No, but he certainly has no shortage of women who'd like to remedy that. His aloofness drives them to distraction. He is impossible to get, so that puts them in a frenzy to get him."

June replied, "Ahhh, this I understand. Age-old technique. I use it all the time in my work. I act like I have absolutely no interest in working for someone. Then, when they realize they're totally dispensable in my book, they have to have *me*. No one else will do."

Kang smiled. "Come to think of it, you and Chris are kind of alike. He's an incredible ladies' man and you're the woman every man would love if he could. And you both have gargantuan egos!"

She lightly slugged him on the arm. "Watch what you say about me, Mr. Seng Kang!"

Two

Among thieves and murderers, there often is a pecking order based on the degree of perceived amorality. A man whose deep evil is apparent can inspire fear even in the most of vile characters. John Pate, a swarthy brawny man with thick black hair and overly large ears, was such a man. But on this night, Pate was in relatively good spirits and was even being social. His lawyers had just successfully defended him against a rape charge, so he was celebrating by playing pool and drinking beer in a seedy bar. He was recounting how he'd beaten the rap.

"Well, being as you're my best buddies, I'll let you in on my little secret. The Kobi Bryant case did us all a great big favor. If a bitch accuses you of rape, you just insist on the evidence from the rape kit. If she's spread for anyone else in the few days prior, then her goose is cooked. You just say it's consensual and she can't prove otherwise."

Another pool player asked whether there wouldn't be bruises and if that wouldn't indicate lack of willingness. Pate replied, "Well, I told them she sure seemed to be likin' it at the time!" The men all laughed.

One asked, "So, how many convictions you beaten all together?"

Pate snorted. "You mean in this state? Don't know. Not keeping count."

Indeed, Pate had an extraordinary record, but had only received one prison sentence and that had been for seven years, of which he'd only served two. Pate was bragging about this when an aging barmaid entered the pool room carrying a tray of beer bottles. Her uniform had been designed for a younger woman. She was wearing a short skirt and low-cut blouse that fully revealed her wrinkled, brown-splotched skin. She was haggard and harried.

She set the tray down and said, "Here you are fellas. I gotta collect for the four rounds now. Gotta close out because I'm off. Who's payin'?"

The men fell silent as they watched Pate, who, leering, stepped toward her. She tried to step away, but Pate grabbed her arm.

"Well now, honey, being as you're off, what do you say you an' me get it on?"

The barmaid jerked away, rubbing her arm. "Keep your paws off me. I'm not your honey and I wouldn't get it on with you if you were the last *homo sapiens* alive."

All the men laughed loudly except Pate, who reacted angrily. He stood over her menacingly, his fists clenched. "What'd you say, bitch?"

A man named Turner tried to defuse the situation, telling Pate to take it easy. He turned to the rest of the men, "Come on guys, pony up. Let's buy Pate's beer for him."

He then took Pate's arm and tried to draw him away. Pate shoved Turner backward, but the others caught him before he fell. Several pulled out money and paid the barmaid, who left the room both angry and frightened.

Everyone but Pate began drinking the beers. Pate was sullen. Sensing that Pate was on the verge of more violence, Turner decided it was time to leave. "Okay, guys, thanks for the game. I gotta get home or my wife will be hopping mad."

Pate snarled, "Fuck your wife."

All the men fell silent and looked at Turner. Turner badly wanted to leave and not fight Pate, but he felt trapped. His buddies would always remember his cowardice if he didn't stand up to Pate. So, Turner set down his bottle and picked up a pool cue by the thin end. His eyes narrowed as he tensed to attack. Pate sneered and began to roll up his right sleeve.

All the men knew Turner didn't stand a chance up against Pate. One of them appealed to Turner, "Come on, man. Pate didn't mean nothing. He's just edgy. You know, the court case and all. Let it go."

Another turned to Pate, "Hey, Pate, tell him you didn't mean nothing."

Two of the men took each of Turner's arms and hustled him out of the bar. Pate grabbed his full beer bottle and smashed it against the wall. He stalked out.

***

Later that night, Pate entered his house and turned on a light in the kitchen. He took a beer from the refrigerator, opened it, and set it on the counter. He headed down the dark corridor to the toilet.

He turned on the bathroom light, belched loudly, and started to pee. Meanwhile a light went on in the bedroom at the end of the corridor.

When Pate exited the bathroom, he noticed the light and stood with a quizzical expression. He was certain it hadn't been on when he'd got home. He cautiously approached the bedroom.

Pate looked in and, seeing nothing, walked into the middle of the room and looked all around. He shook his head, then turned around to go back to the kitchen. He jumped with surprise.

In the doorway stood a figure dressed completely in black, including a black ski mask. In one gloved hand was a gun and in the other, a taser.

Pate exclaimed, "What the hell?"

The woman in black said with authority, firmness, lack of emotion, "I have a taser and a nine-millimeter. I am ambidextrous and am good. Do exactly as I say. Take off your shirt."

Pate grinned broadly, "Hey, a babe! Sure, I'll take my shirt off. But how about we take your shirt off first?"

He started forward, reaching out his hands. A blast from the taser felled Pate, who let out a yelp. She stood still, waiting for him to recover, then said, "Now, stand up slowly and take off your shirt."

When Pate complied, she ordered him to remove his shoes and socks, warning, "If I see one quick move, I fire."

Pate sat on the edge of the bed and complied. She told him to kick his shoes toward the dresser and then to remove his pants. He grinned, fully recovered now.

"Listen, this is goin' a little too far. What's goin' on here?"

He laughed lightly and shook his head, then, suddenly, he lunged. She tased him before he could even take a full step. Pate fell heavily. He was slower to get up this time.

"Let's try that again. Take off your pants. Strip!"

When he'd done so, she told him to lie down on the bed. He paused, seeming to contemplate trying another attack. She motioned toward the bed with the taser. Pate slowly laid down, covering his genitals with his hands.

"See the rope attached to each head post? Place one hand through the noose at the end of each rope."

Pate noticed the ropes for the first time. Recognition that this was all planned worried him. He started to sit up again.

"Do as I say now!"

When he'd done it, she continued, "Good. Now jerk your wrists upward so that the nooses tighten on your wrists."

Pate gently pulled the nooses. He tried to hide with his hands the fact that they were still loose.

"Want another dose?"

Pate pulled the nooses tight. Sweat began to form on his brow and he was visibly worried. Being naked, prone and tied had a significant effect on him. Slightly hysterically, he cried, "Who are you? What d'you want? Why're you doin' this?"

"Good questions. We'll get to all that. But first, I want you to cross your left leg over your body and touch the opposite corner of the bed."

When he'd complied, she laid the nine-millimeter down, keeping the taser in her other hand. Gingerly, keeping well away from Pate's foot lest he try to kick out, she leaned and lifted up a rope with a noose. She dropped it over Pate's right foot and drew it tight, then went to the other corner of the bed and did the same with Pate's left foot. His left hand was now tied to the same side of the bed as his right foot, and vice-versa. She laid the taser beside the gun.

"Now we can talk. You'll notice that you have a great sense of fear. I've used power to overwhelm you and to put you in a position where you can do nothing to help yourself. You keep thinking, 'This can't be happening to me. Something is going to happen to save me.' But it won't. I will do whatever I want to you, and you can do nothing about it. No one is going to save you.

Pate's voice was shaky, "Who are you? What d'you want?"

The woman in black spoke somewhat emotionally for the first time. She replied that it didn't matter who she was. Only her purpose and actions mattered. She told him that she wanted him to feel the same pain and fear that his victims had felt.

Pate sneered, "Look, if you're one of the bitches... Sorry, I mean if you're one of the women... I had sex with I can make it right with you."

Having regained her composure, she said very matter-of-factly, "One of the first things we are going to do is to teach you the right vocabulary. Rape and sodomy is what you did, not 'have sex'. Say it. Say, 'I raped and sodomized women'."

She took a step closer to him. His mood had swung; his face was red with rage. He spit, but she ducked it.

He screamed, "Bitch! I'll teach you what rape is. You won't get away with this. Soon as I get free, you'll pay. I'll give you the lesson in rape and sodomy!"

He struggled violently against the ropes, bucking and yanking. She stepped back, watching to be sure that the bonds held. Pate finally stopped, breathing heavily.

He let out a roar of anguish, gritting his teeth.

Watching his face closely, she said quietly to herself, "I can see that you are unable to learn. That's okay. It makes me all the more sure that what I am doing is right. You'll never be anything but a vicious animal."

She left the room. Pate again desperately struggled against the ropes and howled with rage. She returned carrying an empty beer bottle. Almost breezily, she said "Now, let's continue the lesson."

She removed a pack from her back and reached into it. She drew out a container of Vasoline and smeared some onto the neck of the bottle. He watched with a quizzical expression. Then she held the bottle close to Pate's anus. He tried to squirm away, but had little wiggle room. She jammed in the bottle as Pate screeched. She pushed it all the way in until it disappeared. Gradually Pate's screams diminished to whimpers and he began to sob.

"Stop, man! Oh, God! Please! Why?"

"Please stop. Is that what your victims pleaded? Do you even remember?"

Pate sobbed but didn't answer.

She untied Pate's right foot and tied it to the same side of the bed as his right hand, then repeated the process for the left foot. Pate cried out with each movement. He was now tied spread-eagled on the bed.

"John Pate, do you remember Louise Marsh?"

Pate gasped, "Who?"

"That's what I thought. You raped and strangled her. You were sentenced to just seven years for manslaughter, but served only two." She paused, watching for his reaction, but there was none. "And do you remember Lilly James?"

He shook his head, still wincing. Then he said softly and firmly, "I'm gonna kill you. You're as good as dead. But first I'm gonna do to you whatever I did to the rest of them, and more."

"Hmmm. I guess that means you don't remember Lilly James. Well, I want you to know what happened to her. She was a devout Catholic, Pate. After you raped her, she got pregnant. She could not bear the thought of having a child with your genes, so she got an abortion. She was so guilt-ridden, so full of self-loathing."

Pate snarled, "Break my fuckin' heart!"

She continued as if he hadn't spoken, "Her priest rejected her, telling her that she was no longer a child of the Church. She committed suicide, Pate. And it all began with you. She was happy and young before you, and a crushed, empty shell after you. She was my best friend and now she's gone ... because of you."

Pate sneered, "I shoulda killed her."

"The way I see it, you did kill her. And you killed others too, didn't you? Just like Louise Marsh?"

"That wasn't my fault. The bitch wouldn't quit screaming."

She replied, "My guess is that you won't quit screaming either."

She paused and thought to herself that Pate had been pretty loud when she inserted the bottle. It wouldn't do to have a neighbor call the police. But then she concluded that this was the sort of neighborhood in which people were highly unlikely to ever call the police for anything. And besides, she was almost finished. Or, that was, Pate was almost finished.

She drew out a knife from a sheath. Pate saw it and began to scream. With a quick move, she reached out lifted his penis and sliced it off. His screams increased in decibel and pitch. Then he passed out.

***

Sometimes people seem to look like their dogs. Sometimes wives and husbands not only dress similarly, they even look genetically related. But in the case of Dr. John Oban, he looked like where he worked—the morgue. He was as thin as the quality of the florescent lighting, with silver hair that matched the stainless steel tables. The white smock under his translucent plastic apron was the same tint as the tile walls. His skin was almost as pasty bluish white as the cadavers' on which he worked. But most of all it was his demeanor: he seemed to have no life, either in his eyes or his voice.

It was morning, although you couldn't tell that in the windowless room. Oban was finishing up his autopsy on Maria De La Cruz when Chris Coxon and Seng Kang entered.

Kang chirped, "Hey, John, happy Monday. How's the De La Cruz autopsy going?" His attempt to inject cheerfulness into the room failed. Oban always made him want run outside and gulp fresh air.

Oban droned, "I'm just about done. You're right, Chris. She died of asphyxiation. The tape covered her mouth and the swollen tissue and blood from her broken nose prevented her breathing."

Coxon looked at Kang and held out his hand. Kang shook his head resignedly and reached for his wallet. He handed Coxon a twenty-dollar bill.

They asked several questions about whether there were any clues such as hairs or skin under her nails. Oban explained that she'd apparently been bound up early in the attack and had no chance to scratch her assailant. There were no physical clues.

Coxon sighed, "Just like Tate and Kipplinger. Okay, thanks, John."

Oban nodded without looking up and continued working. Kang and Coxon left got on the elevator. Kang bumped his fist lightly against the wall and said, "Neighborhood canvas a wash. No leads in forensics. This is driving me nuts!"

"Yeah, me too. I was thinking last night. I decided I am going to talk to the Department psychologist."

Kang raised his eyebrows. Coxon slugged him softly on the shoulder. "About the case, Kang."

"I thought you didn't believe in that. Didn't you call it 'analysis by psychos'? In fact, you called him Dr. Voodoo."

"Yeah, well, this case is going nowhere fast. I'm ready to try anything. Besides, there's a new psychologist. Maybe this one's better than the old one."

The elevator stopped and the door opened. Kang got off and waved. Coxon pushed the button for another floor. Coxon got off on a floor he'd been to only once or twice. He felt a sliver of trepidation because he had no positive experiences whatsoever with any of the Department psychologists. He hoped that this would be different, but his expectations were low. Still, if it could help with the case, it was well worth the try.

He came to the door marked "S. Scott." He straightened his tie and knocked. He heard a female voice say "Come in." He thought to himself, a woman? He opened the door and stepped in.

"Ms. Scott, Hi, I'm Chris Coxon. I emailed you..." he started.

Sarah Scott stood and walked around her desk, extending her hand. "Sure, Chris. Good to meet you. Yes, I got your message."

She had short, straight brown hair brushed back from her face. She was of medium build, a bit thin, and muscular. What struck people most about her, however, were her pale glacier-blue eyes.

She gestured for him to sit and took the chair across from him, so that there would be no furniture between them. She added, "By the way, it's Dr. Scott, but please call me Sarah."

Coxon apologized, staring intently at her. She was not at all uncomfortable with the silence and returned his gaze. She thought to herself that if he were younger and had longer hair, he'd look like a living version of Michelangelo's *David*.

He asked, "Do I know you from somewhere?"

"I don't think so. I'm new to the Department."

Then Coxon remembered and snapped his fingers. "I know. In the gym. You're the karate woman!"

Scott smiled. "Well, I do practice the art, but I'm not sure about the moniker 'karate woman'."

"Yeah, okay. It'll be Sarah, then. Anyway. Did you have a chance to look at the materials I sent over to you?"

"Yes. You asked me to look at the files with two questions in mind. First, whether anything strikes me about the women. Second, whether I could form any working impressions of the killer. Right?"

"Exactly."

Scott picked up her note pad. Coxon leaned back, crossed his legs, and tented his fingers under his chin. He was ready to listen.

"As for the women, I don't see much that isn't obvious. Aside from the fact that they were all attractive young women who lived alone, there is only one commonality in the victims' lives and behavior that I can find."

Coxon raised his eyebrows questioningly, as he'd found nothing in common among them yet.

"As you probably have already noted, they all apparently relied on public transportation. But I see no record here of anyone following up on that angle."

Coxon was surprised. "What? I knew that Kipplinger and De La Cruz took the bus. But Tate had a car."

"True, but there is one report ..." Scott rose and went to the credenza behind her desk and retrieved a sheaf of papers. "Yes, here it is. It's a report by a Detective Summerfeld who interviewed Tate's father. He said her car was in the shop for a couple of weeks before she was killed and he thinks she took public transportation to work, but he wasn't sure. Now maybe someone gave her a ride during that time, or maybe she took the bus. It should be easy to check."

"That's pretty damned good. That went right by me, even though I had them interview the body shop boys to see if there was anyone of interest there. I just didn't focus on the bus angle."

He paused for a long moment, then said softly, more to himself than to her, "So our guy might be a bus rider."

Scott replied, "Well, actually, I suspect not. I think our guy is pretty insecure and wouldn't feel comfortable in open surroundings. Also, in the cases of Tate and Kipplinger, they were assertive women who probably would not have hesitated to react publicly if they had felt threatened by anyone following them or bothering them on the bus."

She paused to see if he wanted to make any comment, then continued, "The bus angle might be important because it would be more likely for him to be able to reliably find and follow his victims without loitering in a neighborhood."

They sat in silence. She wanted to give him time to follow up before she changed the subject. When he said nothing, she proceeded, "Before we go on, let me ask you something. Is it correct that in the cases of Tate and Kipplinger there's no indication they knew they were in danger? Was there any particular preparation, like in the case of De La Cruz moving the furniture?"

"No. In fact, the opposite is true in the case of Kipplinger. She was the first. Her window on the ground floor of her townhouse was apparently unlocked. All the guy had to do was pop the screen. Why?"

"I think the murderer probably started out being unknown to his victim. But with De La Cruz, and maybe even Tate, he stalked. This guy enjoys the terror of his victims and he's very likely to stalk the next one. His next victim will probably be aware of him and may even report him."

"Help me with his mind set. I mean, I know he wants to rape them, but what else can you tell me?

"I have a lot more thinking to do on this, but I do have a couple of thoughts for whatever they're worth now."

Scott pulled three pictures out of the file and laid them side-by-side on the desk. Each shows hands tied behind the back. She tapped each. "Their hands are tied behind their backs before the assault. The obvious clue is that the perp used the same type of tape and the figure eight each time. But my interest is in not just what he did, but why he did it. Why did he tie them up early? One possibility is that he's small in stature and strength. Or maybe he doesn't find struggle particularly exciting."

"He enjoys instilling terror, but doesn't like the fighting?"

"Possibly. But he's becoming more violent and he's gaining confidence. Now, you might say murder is the ultimate violence, but obviously there are different levels associated with different means of murder. Tate and Kipplinger were strangled after, or while, being raped. He not only smashed De La Cruz's face in, he stabbed her post-mortem. It's possible that she kicked him or did something to set him off dramatically, but my guess is that he is beginning to let himself enjoy the violence more as his confidence grows."

"He ties them so they can't fight, but he is still violent with them."

"He likes to give it, not get it." She paused. "Now going back to why he tied them up early. His own physical stature may be a reason, but also my guess is that he wanted to make sure that they didn't scratch him. He understands DNA and forensics."

"So, its possible he may have been prosecuted before, perhaps has even served time."

"Or he just watches the right TV shows." She waited a moment, then added, "Also, I didn't see anything in the files about checking the shower. He almost certainly got De La Cruz's blood on him and if he is DNA-savvy, he wouldn't want that on his clothing. He might have showered at De La Cruz's. It might be too late, but it might be worth looking for a towel. Maybe he took it with him, maybe he didn't. And if he did take it, that might be a trophy to look for if we ever get a suspect." He nodded.

She smiled and concluded, "I'll continue to think on this, and I hope you'll send me anything new on the case. I will try to help."

They stood and shook hands. He started for the door, then hesitated but didn't turn back to her.

Scott asked, "Anything else, Detective?"

He turned and looked back at her. "No. No. Thanks for the help, and nice meeting you."

As he reached for the door handle, she said, "Oh, I thought you were going to ask me to have coffee sometime to discuss the case further."

He turned again to look at her. She smiled. He seemed surprised, then amused. "No, actually, I was thinking of asking you to have a drink sometime and *not* discuss the case."

"That would be delightful. Give me a call."

He smiled and left. Walking down the hall past a row of cubicles, he was thinking about how forward she was, yet without seeming brash. "That's a lady who gets what she wants," he murmured. He stopped, laughed out loud and shook his head to himself. Why not? He saw a secretary at her desk and walked over to ask if he might use her department phone directory.

The secretary handed him the book. He looked up the number for the Department psychologist and dialed it on his cell. When she answered, he said, "Hello, Sarah? It's Chris. Would you like to have dinner sometime? Maybe next Friday?" He paused. "Well, how about you meet me when you finish that? I'll text you with a restaurant name and address. What's your cell number?

*****

Coxon headed for Kang's office. When he stuck his head in the doorway, Kang, on the phone, motioned enthusiastically for him to come in and sit down. He finished the phone call and then said, "You're not going to believe this, Chris. I was going through the Tate file and..."

Coxon finished the sentence, "She took the bus the week before she was killed."

"Right! The bus company's emailing me over the schedule for the buses that would connect her townhouse area with where she worked. So, how'd you know?"

"The shrink pointed it out to me."

"He read the interview with Tate's father?"

"*She*. She read the report."

"She? So, is our new shrink good-looking?"

"Not like June, but she isn't bad. But she seems very smart, very interesting. Anyway, I asked her to dinner on Friday."

Kang raised his eyebrows. "Call her Sarah already? Smart? Interesting? And you asked a woman out whose profession is not the oldest? And didn't you tell me never to get involved with someone at work?"

"Button it, Kang."

Just then, Detective Garcia appeared in the doorway. His dour expression belied his message. "Good news, guys. Just got the results from last night's canvas at the De La Cruz bus stop. Woman who takes the five-twelve saw the car. She pegged it. He drives a blue Camaro. Probably a 1983."

Kang looked skeptical. "Yeah, that's fantastic news. But with the number of car types on the road today, how on earth can anyone ID it that narrowly? I don't know anybody that can keep up with car body forms, let alone the year."

Garcia nodded. "But this one was easy. Woman who saw it used to own the same model and year herself. The bad news is that she couldn't see the driver from where she was standing, so no description of him."

Garcia ambled away just as Coxon's cell rang. He looked at the incoming number and took the call. He listened for a few moments then asked, "What's the address?"

He motioned to Kang, who opened his cell ready to enter the address.

"4352 Ocotillo Avenue." He pointed to Kang, who nodded, thumbing in the address.

"Okay. Thanks. Be right there."

When he hung up, explained to Kang that there'd been another murder, this one of a male. They headed for the scene.

***

They drove up to a small house on a cul-de-sac in a very run down neighborhood. None of the houses had lawns, just dirt and weeds. There was litter everywhere. A yellow crime scene tape had been strung, behind which stood a small crowd of curious neighborhood kids.

As they approached the front door, a uniformed cop was puking in bushes. A second uniformed officer sat on steps with his head between his knees, dry heaving.

Kang said, "Wow, this must be a good one for you two to be losing it. What is it, the sight, the smell, or both?"

The one on the steps replied, "Both. Nothing like it, ever."

Kang's cell rang and he stopped to take the call while Coxon proceeded into the house. He walked slowly through the kitchen, pausing to survey the scene. The smell of death and decay was strong. He followed the sounds of conversation toward the bedroom. In the doorway, he paused, repulsed.

Three masked forensic technicians were at work dusting and sampling. A masked photographer was taking pictures of the body. Coxon leaned to look closely at Pate's bloody groin.

Coxon asked, "Did you find his dick?"

A technician replied, "No, not yet."

Coxon said, "There's one full bottle of beer on the kitchen counter. It's possible that the victim didn't know he had company when he arrived home. But I don't see any overt signs of B & E, so have a look and let me know what you find." The technician nodded.

Kang entered. "Oh, Buddha!" he exclaimed.

Coxon turned to him. "Why can't you just say, 'Oh, God' like everyone else?"

Ignoring him, Kang peered closely at Pate's groin. "What is this, a sex crime? A love gone bad? His dick getting cut off like that! Did he cheat on the killer?"

The uniformed cop who'd vomited entered the room still looking queasy. "Detectives, he's John Pate. Long sheet. One of his poker buddies got worried when he didn't show up for a game. Came over this morning to see if he was okay. He smelled the corpse from outside and thought he'd better call 911."

"Okay, thanks. Why don't you wait outside and make sure the poker buddy doesn't leave?" Coxon suggested.

The cop nodded gratefully and left. Coxon squatted down, peering at the rope burns on Pate's ankles, noting that the killer had removed the ropes from the scene. He told the photographer to get good shots of the ankles and wrists. He also instructed close ups of the blood on Pate's chin.

Kang pointed at two sets of tiny wounds on Pate's chest. "Chris, I think those are taser marks." Coxon nodded and asked the photographer for extra shots of the spots.

Coxon turned to another of the technicians and asked, "Can I touch him yet?"

Getting the okay to touch the body, Coxon donned gloves and opened Pate's mouth. He reached his fingers in and pulled Pate's penis out of his mouth. Coxon and Kang looked at each other.

Coxon said, "Oh, Buddha!"

Kang said, "Oh, yuck. His prick is in his mouth." He paused a beat then said, "You know, this reminds me of a joke."

Coxon looked at him askance. "This reminds you of a joke? Jesus, Kang!"

Kang began in the best southern drawl he could muster, "Yeah, there's this good ole Georgia boy, Sam, talking to his good friend Joe-Bob. They're watching Sam's bulldog lick his privates real good. Joe-Bob watches enviously and then says, 'Man, I sure wish I could do that. Looks like it would feel real good.' Ole Sam looks at Joe-Bob incredulously and says, 'Whoa, Joe-Bob, you wouldn't want to do that! Why that bulldog would bite you!'" He drew out the word *bite*.

Coxon slowly shook his head. The forensic technicians chuckled, relieved to have a break from the mood of the scene.

Coxon held up the penis. "Better bag this separately so it won't get lost."

***

Later in the day back at the office, Coxon was doing paperwork when Kang entered. "How's it going?"

Coxon replied tiredly, "Nothing's turned up on the search for someone with a criminal record and a blue Camaro. I don't know...maybe the witness was wrong about the color or the year. Or maybe it's registered in another state. Anyway, they are working on it. What about you?"

"I finished the workup on the Pate murder. That guy was a menace. Several charges of rape that were dropped. Guess he somehow intimidated the victims to let it go. Then one stuck. He was tried for rape and manslaughter of a woman who was found suffocated. Chain of evidence problems, so got light sentence and was released early."

"Let's get someone to place calls to see if there's a record that he did anything to any of his cell mates."

"Yeah, okay." Kang sat on the corner of the desk. "Remember what we were talking about the other day?

About the differences in victims? Well, this is the perfect example."

"Pate versus De La Cruz? About how we should spend more effort on finding the perpetrators of the 'nice' people versus the rats?" Coxon used his fingers to indicate quotation marks around the word *nice*.

Kang nodded. "Exactly. Pate. I mean what good riddance! We should find his killer and pay the dude to get rid of a few more rats."

"Kang, you don't mean that, and I didn't hear it."

"Come on, let's be honest here. Pate was an animal who kept getting off the hook. He served almost no time, although he should have been put away for life. Are you telling me that you have just as much interest in finding Pate's killer as you do in finding who murdered Maria De La Cruz?"

"It's my job ... it's our job ... to find both. And we can't let a vigilante settle the score."

"Well, my interest in finding Pate's killer is more one of curiosity to see who it is rather than assuring justice for Pate."

Garcia stuck his head around the door. "Hey, Chris. Thought you'd like to hear. You asked me to check on whether there were any recent similar murders, you know, a guy getting his privates sliced off. Turns out there is something. Three years ago, out in Portland, there was an ex-con who got it that way."

Coxon asked, "Oregon or Maine?"

"Oh, Oregon. I've asked for the sheet on the victim to check whether he did sex crimes. Should be here tomorrow. See ya."

Garcia disappeared. Kang stood and stretched. Coxon smiled at him and warned, "So about what we were saying, you'd better keep those feelings to yourself, partner. Won't do you any good, come promotion time."

Kang gave him the thumbs up and replied flippantly, "You're the only one I'll tell my secrets to."

***

Later that evening, Coxon met one of his escort women for a drink. She was a young dyed-platinum blond, well made up and sexily dressed. Men at tables around them gave her appreciative looks.

Coxon, sipping a scotch, asked, "So, what's new with you? What'd you do today?"

"Oh, went shopping, had lunch with the girls, the usual sorts of things. I watched TV this afternoon. There's this really great soap I like that has..." She saw that Coxon was not listening. He was pensive, looking past her.

She smiled charmingly. "I'm not sure that you heard a word I said. What's on your mind?"

Coxon refocused, smiling wanly. He looked down at his glass, then pushed it away and looked at her. "Read any good books lately?"

"Books?"

"Yeah, you know, pages between covers that..." He paused, placing his palms on the table. "Look, I'm sorry about that. I think I am not good company right now."

She touched his arm smiling, trying her best to look enticing. "Why don't we go to your place?"

Coxon looked at her, then reached a conclusion. He gently shook his head. "Look, I think I gotta head back to work. Don't take this personally. I'll see you another time."

He stood, took some bills out of his pocket and folded them into her hands, kissing them. He kissed her cheek and walked out of the bar.

Outside, Coxon checked his watch. It was seven o'clock. He took out his cell phone and dialed.

"Hello, Sarah? Chris. Have you got a minute? Are you in a place where you can talk?" He paused. "Okay, I'll make it brief. You remember I told you yesterday about the murder and mutilation of John Pate? Do you think one of his rape victims is likely to have done it? Specifically, do any of women at the crisis center where you volunteer ever discuss doing such as this?"

She replied that she thought it pretty unlikely that they could even if they wanted to. "From what I read, Pate was big and strong. Few women could take him on. And, no, I have never heard anyone suggest that they're going to seek revenge that way."

"Okay, thanks. I'm trying to decide whether to expend resources looking at his past victims. They, their brothers, fathers, boyfriends—it makes for a time-consuming task."

"Well, you're spot-on to assume that it is a crime of sexual punishment. The bottle up his anus is pretty much revenge in kind. But unless you find a clue from the scene that would lead you to somebody, just interviewing past victims and their relatives is unlikely to get you very far."

"Yeah, that's about what I conclude. Okay, thanks. See you."

***

June and Kang loved to go out for brunch on the weekend, often to a café that served wonderful eggs benedict. They sat late Saturday morning eating breakfast and talking about Pate's demise.

"So, like, somebody tied the guy up and sliced it off? Wow. A crime of true passion and thought."

Kang was puzzled. "Why do you say 'crime of thought'?"

"Whoever did it, thought it out in advance. You said Pate was a big bruiser of a guy right, a violent sort? So, somebody had to think about how to do it so that they'd succeed and not get hurt themselves."

"And what'd you mean, 'passion'?

"I just meant that it required true and deep emotion to kill that way."

She could see he didn't understand her. "Look, if you want to hurt a guy before you kill him, you do stuff like kneecap him, right? Or, cut off his fingers or ears, right? I mean, isn't that what's typical?"

"Yeah, I guess. If people get tortured before they are killed, it is usually like you say. But so what kind of person do you think would do this? Was this the result of a lovers' quarrel, or did the killer even know the victim? What's your scenario?"

They ate in silence for a few moments. Then June leaned back in her chair and said conclusively, "I think a woman did it. She was seeking revenge against the guy for what he did to her."

Kang was surprised. He put down his fork and gave her his full attention.

"A woman? Come on, a woman wouldn't do that! ... Would she? And how the hell would she overpower this big bully? And what kind of woman would cut off a man's dick?"

"Seng, think about it. If someone raped me, I'd sure like to cut off his offending little pecker. Like, just putting him in jail doesn't do it for me."

"Jeez, June, I think I'm learning some scary stuff about you!"

"Oh, get a grip. If some guy raped me, I wouldn't have to go after him. You'd beat me to it."

"Damned sure!" Kang was thoughtful for a few moments, then continued, "But if I were going to avenge you, I don't think it would ever occur to me to chop off the guy's penis. I'd beat the hell out of him, for sure, but cutting him up would not be something that would occur to me."

"That's my point. The person who murdered Pate was Pate's victim. Maybe there is a woman out there ... maybe one of this guy's victims didn't have anyone to avenge her."

"You know, one of the million things I love about you is that you give me perspective. You may not be right, but at least you've made me think about it from new angle."

***

That same Saturday morning, Sarah Scott was beginning her volunteer work at the rape crisis center. Several women were seated around a waiting room when Scott entered. She smiled and beckoned a thin young woman named Gina to follow her through a door leading to a small office.

Scott sat at the table and motioned Gina to sit across from her. Scott was relaxed; Gina was sad and tense. "So, Gina, tell me how you have been since last week."

"I still can't sleep much, don't want to eat, can't smile. I can't seem to do much of anything but cry." Gina's eyes welled with tears. She had a hard time continuing. Her voice broke as she said, "I keep thinking that the tears will run out and I will get on with my life, but it isn't working. I still feel so dirty. I shower over and over, but the filth doesn't go away."

"Gina ... look at me please. Gina, it has been only a few weeks since you were attacked. You aren't going to get over this in the blink of an eye. It takes time."

Gina began to cry in earnest. Scott handed Gina a tissue and leaned forward to put a hand on her arm. "Gina, whose fault was the attack?"

"I know what you want me to say. You ask me this every time. But I can't get it out of my mind that I shouldn't have gone to the rodeo, that I shouldn't have been in the wrong place."

"Gina, you have every right to have gone to the rodeo. Every woman has the right to do so. If we were to take what you are saying as valid, women would have to hide indoors and never go out."

"I feel terrible inside. I think over and over, what if I hadn't been there? What if ... I don't know."

"That's a natural reaction when anything terrible happens to someone. We all do what you are doing. We think that maybe if we had done just one thing differently, or at a different time, the bad incident would not have happened."

She is unsure whether Gina is truly hearing her. "Gina, there is no way to change the past, but you can shape your future. You can dwell on this and let it rule your life, or you can say you won't let what this criminal, this animal, did to you rule your life."

"Dr. Scott, I say the words, but the meaning is not in my heart. Oh, God, how I hate him. I hate that man!"

"Good. That's totally valid. It is okay to hate him. What is not okay is to blame yourself for the rape."

"And I feel like I am from Mars or something. I tried to talk about it with a friend, but she acted like I should just bury it."

"No, you shouldn't bury it. Quite the opposite. Your friend just doesn't relate to what happened to you. That is why I would like for you to come to the support group. There you can talk with women, and even men, who have endured what you have. They get it. They've been where you are. Do you think you are ready for that yet?"

Gina nodded. Scott explained to her how often the sessions would be, what to expect, and ushered her to the door. Scott counseled several more victims.

At 5:30, Scott reached for her purse and texted Uber to come pick her up. Then she left to meet Coxon at a Thai restaurant.

***

Scott entered the restaurant and stood at the entrance searching to see if he were already seated. She spotted him in a corner booth talking animatedly with the waitress about the menu. She thought to herself that he was one of the most attractive men she'd seen in a very long time. She vowed to herself that wherever this relationship took them, she was going to enjoy it to the hilt.

She started for the table. He spotted her when she was halfway across the room and stood to greet her. She noted that he shook hands rather formally when he could have kissed her cheek. When they were seated, he explained that his partner Kang had recommended this place and had even suggested what they should eat and drink.

"Would you like to go with that, or would you prefer to choose from the menu yourself?" he asked.

She agreed to go with Kang's recommendation, including the wine. The waitress smiled and went to fill the order while they made small talk.

Then Scott said, "So, I have a confession."

"So early? We just got here, and this is our first date!"

"It's just a small confession. I've been asking around about you and I found out you're an artist."

"That's it? That's no secret."

"True, but now at least I know something about you. Actually I never would have guessed it. I love it when I am surprised."

"You know, I don't tell many people. They seem to look at me differently when they learn that I sculpt. I guess they think it's aberrant behavior for a cop."

He explained that his mother had been an artist and how he'd played in her studio as a boy, learning very early the mechanics of how sculpting is done. His mother had encouraged him and by the time he was a teenager, he'd already begun making money from art sales.

Sarah was intrigued. "I want to see your work sometime. That is, if you are willing to show me. But tell me, how do you get the time to do it with your job and all?"

He said he felt he never had enough time for either of them, but he knew if he were to focus exclusively on one, he would get bored. "Also, I see them as complementary. Art frees my mind and relaxes me. It's kind of like getting a mental recharge so that I can be a better detective. I liken it to getting a good night's sleep: when I do, I am much more productive."

The waitress brought the wine and he tasted it. He indicated he'd like for Sarah to taste it as well. She liked that he treated her as a partner in the decision. She nodded that she liked it. When the wine was poured, and the waitress had left he proposed a small toast: "Let's drink to success." She liked that too; it meant everything and nothing.

"So, what're we having to eat?"

"We are starting with a couple of seared scallop salads with miso dressing. A pause after that, then we'll split the Thai chicken curry with extra lime and cilantro. You know, I used to be stuck on finding the best burger in town. Now Seng has me eating all kinds of things. He's quite the gourmand."

They discussed food for a few moments, but he wanted to talk about her. He asked about her past and why she worked for the Department. She told him that she'd been a junior detective in Hillsboro, Oregon.

"I probably got the job because they needed a woman for the spot. But then I got really interested in how the bad guys think. I wanted to understand the psychological side of things rather than the physical and logistical aspects. So, I left the department and went back to school for my PhD. I attended UT Austin, so it seemed logical to try for a spot here when I'd finished. I really like the town."

"So, tell me, Doctor, Where do you stand on the 'its in your genes' versus 'you learn it' theories of what makes a criminal?"

"Nature versus nurture? It's both, for sure. If someone is going to be a criminal as an adult, they almost certainly will manifest aberrant behavior as a youngster."

"So, we could just round up the kids that pull wings off of butterflies, stick a label on them, and keep them under observation to prevent crime?"

"No, that wouldn't work. Aside from the impracticality of that, the likelihood of mistakes in judgment and conclusion about who gets labeled could be catastrophic. And, even if someone is a bad seed in youth, sea changes are possible."

"A zebra can change its stripes?" he asked skeptically.

"It's happened. In school one of our case studies was a teenaged patient in the early 1960s. The boy was physically ugly. Had a big nose, huge adam's apple. And he was miserable. Thought everyone hated him, particularly girls, and he hated himself. He was beginning to act aggressively and started getting in trouble. Then suddenly the Beatles hit. This kid just so happened to look a lot like Ringo Starr. He grew his crew cut out into a mop top, started wearing mod cloths and rings on his fingers. The girls went crazy for him, and he became genuinely popular. He was young enough that his personality could still grow, so he handled the sea change well. The kid was cured."

"So do you think a sea change can occur with a guy like the one who killed Maria De La Cruz?"

"No way."

"That's what I think too."

"So do you think that there's a prerequisite that criminals be ugly?"

She laughed. "It almost seems that way, but no. I think handsome people are represented among criminals in about the same proportion that they make up the general population. Having said that, being unattractive can certainly contribute to the insecurity that fuels a lack of self-esteem, which is definitely a criminal characteristic."

They continued to dine and talk about work. He was very interested in learning about the psychology of rapists and asked many questions. She told him about the use of rape as a weapon in war and how it is more common in patriarchies. He was particularly stunned at the statistic that up to 50% of women experience rape during their lifetime in some western African countries.

At one point, Coxon summed up, "So we can't talk about the psychology of rapists in general, we have to discern which type of rapist—whether it is a date rape, a gang rape, rape by soldiers in war, or rape by a psychopath."

"While there will be commonalities among those groups that we can identify, you are essentially correct. Studies have shown that psychologically disturbed men are more stimulated by images of sexual activity involving violence, whereas 'normal' men have the opposite response. And it is important to factor in that misogyny is often the result of a childhood trauma inflicted by a woman."

The conversation still intrigued him after dinner, so he asked if she'd like one more glass of wine. When it came, he asked her how she liked the Department so far. She told him that she spent most of her time on two things, evaluating potential employees and counseling people who'd been victims of crime. She hoped that in the future she would become more involved in casework. In that regard, she thanked him for the opportunity to work on his case. He offered that she'd be welcome to come to their morning 8:30 AM briefings if she had the time.

At the end of the evening, he took her arm as they left the restaurant and stood with her outside while she awaited Uber. When the car came, he helped her in but didn't kiss her on the cheek. She thought to herself that, for a man with a reputation of being a ladies' man, he certainly was reserved.

THREE

On Monday afternoon, George Lehman was again parked across from the bus stop where he'd previously seen a woman that interested him. He'd already followed her home a couple of times, so he knew where she lived. But he had not let her see him the way he had with the Mexican woman. As much as he enjoyed seeing the fear he could engender, he had concluded that it was too dangerous for the women to see him in advance. He had not liked it that the Mexican woman had tried to block the doors with furniture. After all, the thought, what if one of his targets built herself a little fortress more effectively? So he'd changed his tactic; he tracked them from a little more distance.

As he waited, he was becoming impatient. He checked his watch and knew that she'd appear any moment. And then, there she was.

Marilyn Cummins was a slightly heavy, very pretty woman with a wide face and fulsome lips. She was well dressed and coiffed. She arrived at the bus stop and put on her iPod, swaying gently with the music she was listening to.

Lehman watched her intently, thinking how much of a snob she must be. The thought of being with her excited him so much that he wanted to move up the time of his event with her.

That was another new aspect this time around—he felt more urgency and sooner. With the first two women, he had been able to enjoy the afterthought of them for much longer before he felt compelled to seek another victim. It had occurred to him once that he might be able to pace events better and prolong his pleasure between events if he brought something home with him—a photo, a trinket, some underwear, or something. But he knew better than to do that. He knew he had to be ultra careful so that he could maintain deniability in case there was ever a mistake. But, then, he didn't plan on making mistakes.

The bus came and Lehman watched her board. Then he followed from a distance until she got off and went into her house.

Lehman felt agitated. He tried to think of something to do with himself so that he could calm down. He went for a soda, he drove around aimlessly, filled his car with gas, but then he found himself at the grocery store where Cummins usually shopped. He knew he was becoming almost ill with his preoccupation with her.

Lehman went home and stood in the center of his room, breathing deeply with his eyes closed. He lit a cigarette and sat in his chair smoking. Soon he realized it was pointless to try to postpone the event.

He walked the dresser, opened a drawer, and took out a pair of latex gloves. He began his routine of wiping items down and placing them in his black fanny pack. He stood staring at the pack for a few moments until his breathing became calm. Then he slowly stripped, folding his clothing neatly as he went. He went to the bathroom to shave his body and shower. He dressed in fresh black clothes and then turned off the lights and sat, again smoking and waiting. He had the routine down.

He so enjoyed these moments beforehand. He went over in his mind the last event, the one with the Mexican girl. She'd almost made it through the window when she tried to run. He wouldn't ever let that happen again. But he wished she hadn't died so quickly. He vowed to be more careful so that everything would last longer next time. Also, he had to keep blood off of their faces. He wanted to see their eyes clearly.

Then he thought about tonight. This girl was just like the other three. She thinks she's so beautiful and above it all, "but she isn't" Lehman said aloud. Their make-up is so perfect, they dress so well, their hair is just right, he thought to himself. They're the kind who would always look down on him, but he would have the last laugh. He would look down on them.

At last, it was late enough. He asked himself if he shouldn't wait a couple of more hours, like he had before. Then he could be fairly sure that she was asleep. But, no, he was too eager. He decided he didn't really care if she were soundly asleep.

He got up and put on the fanny pack. He stood again in the center of the room with his eyes closed in the dark, imagining what was to come. Then he left and drove to Cummins' house. As he had with the other events, he parked several houses away and walked as much as he could in shadows.

Lehman stood behind Cummins' house. He checked his watch; it was ten PM. He donned the latex gloves and inspected the window. He then checked the door in case it would be easier. He was amazed that it was unlocked. This was meant to be, he told himself.

Entering the kitchen, he accidentally bumped a chair. He stood still, listening to see if there would be a response. Upstairs, Cummins was sitting in her bed, reading. She didn't hear the noise.

Lehman relaxed, enjoying being inside her house and the expectation of what was to come. Then he switched on his flashlight and headed for the hallway. A startled cat ran underfoot and screeched as Lehman stepped on it.

Cummins heard it and shut her book. She listened intently, but there was no further sound. She was asking herself whether she should go and investigate. Then a stair creaked.

Without even stopping to think, Cummins quickly reached for the gun in her bedside drawer, checking to make sure the safety was off. She didn't need to check that a bullet was in the chamber because she routinely made sure of that. She stole out of bed, turning off the bedside light. Per her plan laid long ago for such an event, she went into her closet and closed the door quietly.

Lehman had seen the light under the doorway switch off, so he turned off his flashlight and froze in case she opened the door and came out. Soundlessly, he put the flashlight in his fanny pack. Being sure that she was in there and awake thrilled him.

Hearing nothing from her bedroom, he tried the door. The handle turned easily, and he pushed the door inward, making sure that she was not hiding behind it. There was enough moonlight for him to see that the bed was empty.

He began to strip and fold his clothes as quietly as he could. He followed his routine with the tape and condom. Then he set the fanny pack on the dresser with his clothes.

Very gently he said, "I know you're here. Come out and I won't hurt you. Don't be afraid. I promise I won't hurt you." But there was not a sound.

He checked the bathroom, making certain she wasn't behind the shower curtain. Then he turned his attention to the closet. He walked to the door and slowly opened it.

As she heard the handle turn, Cummins squeezed her eyes shut. Both hands were on the gun, and she was shaking with adrenaline and fear. As the door opened, she fired.

Lehman fell backwards, hit in the thigh. He was stunned momentarily. All he could think was, why on earth did she have a gun?

She bolted past him. He grabbed her gown, causing her to stumble and fall. The gun skittered across the floor out of reach. She regained her balance and fled down the stairs and out the front door.

Lehman could hear her shouting and banging on the neighbor's door. He knew he didn't have much time before the police arrived and that there was no way he could be sure that his blood was cleaned from the scene in time. He decided to leave and figure out what to do about this later.

He hurriedly put on his clothes, struggling to get a pant leg over his wounded thigh. Having checked that his fanny pack was intact and that he was leaving nothing but his blood, he limped downstairs and exited the back door.

He could see the light on the porch of the neighbor's house. His car was in the opposite direction.

By the time he reached his car, Lehman was worried about how much blood he was losing. He took a rope he kept in the car and tightened it around his thigh. He knew he had no choice but to seek medical attention. He had the presence of mind to think that the hospital staff would wonder why there was no bullet hole in his pants, so he took his knife and ripped the pant leg. If they asked him about the tear, he would say he did it in an effort to staunch the flow of blood.

The route to the hospital took him over the river. On the bridge, he unfastened his fanny pack and threw it out the window into the water. He then peeled off the gloves and tossed them too.

He parked at the hospital and started limping toward the door. He felt faint, but made it inside.

***

Cummins sat on her neighbor's sofa, dressed in a man's large robe. The police had arrived and had summoned Seng Kang due to the possibility that the event could possibly be another involving the serial rapist.

When Kang arrived, the uniformed officers briefed him in the kitchen about what they'd learned. Kang knew that any hospital would contact the police about a gunshot wound, be he wanted the uniformed officers to contact the hospitals anyway because this perpetrator might not only be dangerous, but also Kang wanted to be directly informed in this case. He gave them his cell number to pass to the hospital staffs. He also warned them to be careful when entering Cummins' house to look for evidence, as the perpetrator could possibly still be there.

Kang went to interview Cummins. The information was what he'd already heard, but he had a few questions. "Ms. Cummins, whose gun did you use?"

"Mine. It was my grandfather's. Before he died, he gave it to me. 'Always have a bullet in the chamber,' he said, 'because if the time comes to use it, you may not think to put one in'."

"Did you give the man who broke into your house any warning that you would shoot?"

She looked at him in disbelief. She was irritated that there would be a tone that somehow she might be to blame in any of this. "Are you kidding? I was like in fear of my life! He was in my house. He came after me. I wasn't like going to have a fricking conversation with him."

"Do you know where you hit him?"

Cummins' took a deep breath, telling herself to be calm. "No. But I don't think I hurt him too bad. He like came after me and pulled me down."

"Ms. Cummins, do you take the bus regularly?"

"What's that got to do with anything?"

"Please answer my question."

"Yes, it's cheaper you know to ride the bus than to park my car. Why?"

"Have you noticed anyone…"

Kang's cell rang and he walked to the other side of the room to take the call. He listened for a moment and then grinned to himself. He thanked the caller and returned to Cummins. He told her that the officers would get her some clothing from her house and escort her to the precinct to record her statement. He then went outside and placed a call to Coxon.

"Hey, Chris. You still on your date?" He paused and then explained briefly what had happened, ending with, "And I just got a call from General Hospital. He went there. I am on my way. You want to come in case he talks?" Coxon agreed.

***

Kang was waiting in a small lobby outside the hospital emergency room, talking to a uniformed officer when Coxon entered. He smiled at Coxon, "Chris, you're gonna love it. Blue Camaro."

"Anything in it?"

"We took a peek, but there's nothing obvious. We didn't look closely. It'll take awhile to get the warrant."

"You talk to him yet?"

Kang explained that Lehman was still in treatment and that they'd had to give him blood. The nurse had just been out to say that they were almost through with him. Kang added, "And guess what? She says his whole body is shaved!"

They moved over to a coffee machine in the waiting area. Coxon got them two cups and they sat on plastic chairs. Kang recounted everything he'd learned from Cummins.

When they finally had exhausted the subject, Kang asked, "So, how'd your date go tonight?"

"It was good. I like her. And thanks for the recommendation. We both liked the restaurant."

"So is this going anywhere?"

"I doubt it. I don't really need that, you know. I'm just enjoying her, that's all. She's interesting and I like talking with her."

Two nurses entered the hallway pushing Lehman on a gurney. The uniformed officer was following. Coxon and Kang joined the procession. They all entered an elevator, where Kang positioned himself in front of Lehman. "George Lehman, you're under arrest for breaking and entering the…"

Lehman interjected, "I know my rights. I want an attorney right now. Not another word til then."

"Don't you want to tell us what you were doing in Marilyn Cummins' house?"

Lehman sneered at Kang, but remained silent.

"Why'd she shoot you?" Coxon asked.

Lehman turned his face away from them. The doors opened and the Nurses pushed Lehman down the hall into a private room. The uniformed officer stationed himself outside the door. Coxon and Kang stayed outside too.

Kang asked if he should try to get an attorney now. They both looked at their watches. Coxon decided that it was too late now, but they should try to get someone for the following day even though it would be Sunday. They decided to call it a night.

***

The next morning, they met at the hospital with attorney Walter Thornton and thanked him profusely for coming on a Sunday. They then waited for a half hour while he went and consulted with his client, Lehman. Finally, Thornton stuck his head out the door and called them in.

They set up a tape recorder and stated the usual preliminaries. When finally they got to the substance, Coxon asked why Lehman was in Cummins' house.

Lehman replied, "She invited me." He offered nothing else, which was to be his mode the entire interview: offer minimal information.

Coxon and Kang looked at each other in disbelief. Coxon said, "She invited you? When did she invite you?"

After many questions, they recorded Lehman's version of events, which was that Cummins had come up to him the grocery store and started flirting. She then asked him to come to her house. She had suggested 9:00 PM, which he thought was a bit late, but he found it too intriguing to resist.

When he'd gone to her house, she invited him in and they talked for a while. She had said she had to go to her room for something and he sat down to pet her cat. Then she called to him, and he went to her room, a bit hesitantly because he was beginning to suspect she wasn't quite normal. When he went into the room, she shot him.

When Lehman finished his story, Coxon gave Kang a look that said, this is too much! "What motive would she have to shoot you?"

Lehman replied, "No idea. In my book, she's just crazy."

Kang asked, "Did you attack her?"

Lehman said indignantly, "Course not. I was totally taken by surprise. I can't remember much about what happened after being shot, but I remember being afraid that she would shoot me again. I just ran."

Coxon said, "Mr. Lehman, we'd like to take a look around your house and in your car. Would you mind that?"

Thornton intervened, "No way. There are no grounds for that. I think he has answered your questions and that's enough." He paused, then said, "By the way, my client is pressing charges against the Cummins woman for shooting him. I'll be getting to you soon on that. And I think you'll agree that there is clearly no basis for the arrest of Mr. Lehman."

Kang commented to Lehman, "I tell you, bud, you've got chutzpah." They then terminated the interview and the detectives exited.

As they left, Coxon mused that Lehman would probably delay in pressing charges to give Cummins time to decide not to pursue anything against Lehman. "It's just a threat. If she lets it go, he'll let the shooting go."

Kang agreed and said that he'd get the warrant process started. Coxon suggested he also get someone to look into the possibility that Cummins has a record either of shooting someone else or mental instability of any sort. Even if Lehman did look like a bad guy and drove a blue Camaro, they couldn't jump to conclusions, they had to get the evidence step by step.

***

The next day was a slow Monday with only one noteworthy item. A search of government records revealed that Cummins had once gone on disability at the bank where she had worked. She had gotten a psychiatrist to document that she was suffering from extreme stress in her home life due to the deaths of her parents, as well as interpersonal work relationship problems.

The details, other than this skeletal information, were sealed. But it was enough to cause both Coxon and Kang to worry that Lehman might have something to work with in building a case that Cummins attacked him unprovoked. They decided to bring Cummins in again on Tuesday. Coxon told Kang that he might like Sarah Scott to sit in on the interview and Kang agreed, so Coxon called her and set it up.

On Tuesday, they got some mixed news. The judge had granted a warrant for Lehman's car based on the claim made by a witness in the De La Cruz case that a blue Camaro was involved. However, he denied a warrant for Lehman's home. He noted in the denial that it was Lehman who had been harmed, that there was no evidence to suggest that Lehman had attacked Cummins, that Lehman had no record, there was no sign of break-in at Cummins' house, and that there were preliminary indications that Cummins might have a history of instability. When the police searched Lehman's Camaro, they found nothing but his blood and the bloody rope he'd used as a tourniquet.

The interview with Cummins took place in the late afternoon. Coxon and Kang asked her several questions, but when they got to the subject of the disability, she clammed up, saying it wasn't relevant. Cummins said she needed to go to the bathroom and while she was away, Scott asked if she could talk alone with Cummins for a few moments. They agreed.

Scott went to the ladies' room where Cummins was combing her hair and applying lipstick. Scott began talking about how Lehman was a real sleeze, but a smart sleeze. She told Cummins that he was likely to take her to court over the gunshot and that she, Cummins, could have her history dredged up and exposed.

"So listen, Marilyn, I can help, but I really need to know the truth. If you tell me here, we won't have to do it in the formal interview on tape. Can you tell me the truth? Was there anything violent in the psychiatric evaluation done for the disability case?"

Cummins got tears in her eyes. "There was a guy at the bank where I worked who wouldn't let me alone. He'd come up behind me and touch my ass. He was constantly making remarks about my breasts. I complained, but no one would do anything because I think they didn't believe me because he didn't do it in front of anyone."

"Did you finally have enough of it?"

"Yes. One day I just couldn't take it anymore. He came up behind me and ran his finger down my back. I just cracked. I had a pencil in my hand, and I whirled around and stabbed him. It went pretty deeply into his shoulder."

Cummins began to sob. Scott comforted her for a while, then told her that it was best for her to go home. She said she'd tell the detectives. If they had any more questions, they would call her back another time.

When Cummins had left, Scott went to break the news to the detectives that Lehman would probably have a case if he pursued it.

***

Tuesday evening, Coxon headed for the gym. He pushed himself hard and felt exhausted at the end of the workout. His trainer praised his progress. Now he stood with a towel around his neck, staring through the door into the next room where Scott was working with her karate teacher. He loved watching her. She reminded him of a feline, strong and supple.

As Coxon watched her, he felt a twinge of embarrassment that he found himself visualizing a co-worker naked. He wondered to himself whether anyone could tell that he was mentally undressing her if they were watching his face.

Coxon's trainer walked by just behind him and teased that Coxon was spending a lot of time in this particular doorway. Coxon turned to reply, but he'd already walked away. When Coxon turned back to Scott, she had paused the workout and was looking at him. Their eyes met and she smiled ever so slightly. He grinned.

She bowed to her instructor to end the session and approached Coxon. She leaned against the doorjamb opposite him and crossed her arms. She said nothing, but her eyes started from his face, then ran down his body, then back to his face. Her eyes seemed to have a flicker of appreciation.

Coxon couldn't help but let out a laugh. He realized that he'd just been mentally undressed by a co-worker. And, yes, he noted, it is possible to tell that from the look in the viewer's eyes.

Finally, the silence got to him and he searched for something bright to say. "Thanks for helping today. I don't think we could have gotten the info from Cummins easily. You saved us a lot of time."

"My pleasure," she said.

He could tell she wasn't going to add anything to the conversation, but he wanted to keep it going. "So what made you take up karate?"

Scott explained, "I started when I was eight. Three boys pinned me to the ground during recess and threw sand in my eyes. Two teachers stood by laughing. I learned that authorities don't always protect you. When I told my dad about it, he said I needed to learn to fend for myself. So he sent me to karate school. One of the best decisions he ever made for me."

"So did you ever karate chop the three little boys?"

Scott laughed and confessed that she hadn't. Then she surprised him. She asked him if she could reciprocate the nice dinner at the Thai restaurant with a plate of pasta. "How about next weekend, say, Saturday?"

He thought about how he had decided to play it cool with her and wait a couple of weeks before suggesting another date. But faster was fine with him. "Love to. Text me time and color of wine."

She said, "Deal. Goodnight." Then she turned and walked away.

He headed for the locker room feeling pretty good about the ending of an otherwise lousy day. Sarah Scott was feeling good too. It had been a long time since she had felt the electricity of lust.

***

Mark Mannon was a wealthy attorney in his early 50's who was overweight, balding, and had a nose that was way too big for his Slavic face. His abrasive personality served him well in his profession but had helped assure that no marital relationship survived.

He had come home in the evening after a few drinks with his pals and had eaten a whole bag of corn chips while watching a late-night movie on TV. Now he was lying on the bedspread clad only in boxer shorts, asleep and snoring loudly. The bedside light was still on, as was the TV. The bedside clock read 2:00 AM.

In the doorway to the bedroom, the woman in black stood looking at him. She had used a set of lockpicks to open the back door lock and was now preparing to do what she'd come for. But this event would be different from her treatment of John Pate, for Mannon was no murderer.

She set her nine-millimeter and taser on the bedside table. Then, with a quick chop to the back of Mannon's neck rendered him unconscious. Moving rapidly and efficiently, she pulled out a knife and deftly ripped open Mannon's underwear. She swabbed his entire genital area with brown disinfectant. She opened a package containing a sterilized scalpel, then carefully removed Mannon's testicles, leaving them lying between his legs. She covered the wound with impregnated surgical gauze. She then put everything she'd brought with her into the backpack and put it on.

She picked up Mannon's the phone, dialed 911, then hung up when the call was answered. She went to the front door, removed the chain lock, opened the deadbolt, and then exited the back door.

***

The following morning was Friday. Kang was driving with Coxon in the passenger seat. Kang was talking about Cummins. "She is pretty upset about Lehman's story. I didn't advise her, but I think she's not going to press charges. I think she doesn't want anything to come out about that period of disability. But I find it hard to read her."

Coxon replied, "I still believe her side of the story. And I'm still pissed that we couldn't get a warrant to search Lehman's home. The blue Camaro tie-in should have been enough to sway the judge."

"Yeah. But I think the lack of a past on the guy was pretty important. It's unbelievable that the guy's never been arrested. When I saw him, I expected he'd have a long sheet. But nada, zip."

"And there wasn't a mark on her to indicate attack. No sign of forced entry."

They were interrupted by Coxon's cell phone pinging, indicating a text message. He opened the phone, read it and smiled. Kang asked what the good news was.

"Sarah. She wants white wine for tomorrow night's dinner."

"Dinner again? Her place? You falling for her?"

"Don't know."

"You going to sleep with her?"

"Naw. I don't want to rush anything."

Kang had a big smile. "Well, that's it."

"What?"

"You're falling in love with her. You're trying not to move too fast 'cause you don't want to mess it up."

Coxon replied with a noncommittal "Mmm".

Kang changed the subject, telling Coxon about his conversation with June in which she'd opined that a woman probably did the mutilation of John Pate. "Said she'd want to do that to any guy who raped her, if she could. Said guys would probably just seek revenge by beating or killing, not cutting genitals."

"Could be, I guess. But in the case of Pate, Sarah says he's too big and strong. Few women would be able to take him on."

Kang laughed, "Unless they're experts in karate and are well-armed, right?"

Coxon didn't smile. He looked at Kang, who quit smiling. Then Coxon's phone rang.

He took the call and listened for a several moments, then told the caller that they were almost at the office and to please wait for them.

After getting off the phone, he told Kang that a lawyer named Mannon got his balls cut off last night. He was another accused rapist, but one who's never done time.

"He is doing fine, but I guess he won't be a rapist anymore. Garcia wants us to touch base with John Miles, the officer who is most fluent with Mannon's last rape case. Wants us involved because of a possible connection to Pate's murder."

"A little like Pate, but not exactly."

"That's the thinking—mutilation of another rapist. At least this guy's still alive though."

When Coxon and Kang reached the precinct, they were directed to a room where Officer John Miles was waiting for them. Miles described how it was pretty clear to him that Mannon was guilty of rape, but the jury found differently. The history of the case was pretty simple. Mannon and a buddy of his named Waller went to a lesbian bar to make trouble. Started hitting on women and making loud remarks. They got thrown out. A bit later, in the parking lot, they accosted two lesbians who were leaving the bar and raped them both.

Coxon asked for details on the evidence. Miles told him that the DNA was solid and that they'd had a pretty tight case. "But a crafty, very good lawyer can undo even the best case and instill doubt in the minds of jurors it seems." He added that the fact that Mannon was an attorney himself helped in several ways, but the key was his getting his case separated from Waller's. Waller went to prison, but Mannon got off.

Kang couldn't understand how there could be doubt in the jurors' minds if the DNA were solid. Miles explained that the defense focused on the chain-of-custody of the samples from the rape kit and kept questioning whether there had been problems. The defense was able to muddy the waters. They cast enough doubt that the jury was unsure. Miles then paused and said that he didn't want to be quoted, but he would not be surprised to learn that there'd been jury-tampering in the Mannon trial.

Coxon asked how the victims reacted. Miles replied, "You mean do I think they could get together and go cut off his balls? Sure, I think so. And I guess I wouldn't blame 'em if they did."

They thanked him for the summary and asked him to call if he came across anything else relevant.

***

On the following day, Garcia and Kang dropped in to talk with Coxon in his office. Garcia, who was the lead on the Mannon case, noted that the 911 caller must have known that a hang-up would bring a rapid response by the police. They discussed this, plus the fact that the front door had been unlocked. It seemed pretty clear that the care taken to keep the wound clean, plus the 911 call, indicated that the perpetrator was in no way trying to kill Mannon, making it a very different case from Pate's. Garcia was leaning toward thinking that the cases might be unrelated. Coxon didn't buy it, saying that sexual mutilation of rapists was too unusual for the cases to be unrelated.

An officer entered and handed a report to Garcia, then left. Garcia scanned it. "Well, both of Mannon's rape victims are in the clear. They were delighted to hear of his castration, but both of their alibis are good."

Kang said, "Maybe the perp is a Common Joe. Someone just got fed up with people committing rape and getting away with it."

Coxon replied, "Could be. But I get hung up on the notion that Common Joe gets worked up about rape versus other crimes. I mean, what about severe domestic violence, child pornography, even murder? Why go after rapists and not other types of criminals?"

Garcia said, "I'm not sure a Common Joe knows how to castrate so carefully like that. Also, for whatever it's worth, I took a long shot and looked into the question of whether there was one victim of both Pate and Mannon. There wasn't. At least, not one that we know about."

Coxon was growing irritable, which was unusual for him. He threw his pencil onto the desk and said almost angrily, "I can't even think of a next step to take. We've had weeks with no real leads or clues."

Kang knew he was mentally back on the serial killer cases. "Then we just have to wait…"

Coxon cut him off. "I know. I know. We have to wait until the bastard strikes again. We have to wait until a mistake is made."

Cecilia Drake stuck her head in the door and with her ever-merry smile chirped, "Hi, guys! Chris, do you have a minute to look at the press release?"

Coxon barked, "To hell with the goddamn press. We have more important things to do - like solve crimes - than to be spending our time coddling them!"

Drake had an expression saying, "Yikes! What'd I do?"

Kang looked reproachfully at Coxon, then got up and took Drake's arm and steered her out of the room, saying, "I'll take a look at it, Cecilia."

Garcia heaved himself out of the chair and ambled out the door, mumbling "Happy Friday." Coxon wadded up some paper angrily and threw it against the wall.

***

At home that night, Coxon worked on his art. Most people have something that regularly occupies their off-work time. Some watch hours of TV, some read, or whatever. He thought watching the news was meaningless because there was nothing he could do about most of what happened in the world and every story had a spin that assured you'd not really know the facts. And watching most programming was to him mind-numbing. For Coxon, the three to four hours of free time he had in a day were devoted to art, which was not only lucrative, it was fulfilling.

It was well past midnight when he put the finishing touch on a sculpture he'd worked on for the past few months. No sooner had he finished it than thoughts of work overtook him.

He poured himself a scotch and sat in an armchair to think. He was ill at ease about work because he couldn't identify the next steps to take. And something else was bothering him, but he couldn't articulate it. He was beginning to feel something that he worked hard to successfully avoid—stress.

The following day was Saturday. He went to work for a half day to review the criminal record of the man who'd been mutilated and killed in Portland. Like Pate, he'd been accused numerous times of rape, but the charges were always dropped. He decided to call the Portland Department on Monday and see if he could learn anything else about the case.

***

Saturday night, Coxon arrived at Scott's apartment with a bottle of wine. She opened the door as soon as he rang the bell. Once inside, he handed her the wine with a smile, but without a kiss or a hug hello.

Scott looked at the bottle and told him that she loved this particular wine, but then she loved almost any wine produced in Carneros. "But you don't mind starting with champagne first, I hope." He shook his head.

Coxon walked around looking at her apartment, which was spacious and modern, almost spartan. He studied some photos on the wall, then peered at the titles of books on her shelf. He ran his hand over the collection of CDs, considering her taste in music. She watched him walk around the room, touching things, looking. She felt like he was entering her mind, probing her personality.

His first words were, "Nice place."

She thanked him and bustled in the kitchen, which was in full view of the living room, just across an island. She put a dish in the oven and then she popped the champagne and poured two glasses.

She walked to him and extended one, smiling. "Today I felt like a teenager getting ready to have a date over. It was fun cooking for you, getting ready for you. It's been awhile since I had a guest."

He was pensive and didn't return her smile. He reached out and took both their glasses from her and set them on the coffee table. He gently pulled her toward him until they were standing very close.

"Today I was thinking a lot about tonight too. I decided I'd like the evening to begin with how I wish our first date had ended. But at the time, we'd had wine and I didn't want any soft edges on my memory of our first..."

She stood very still. He touched her face softly, running his finger down her cheek. Then he pulled her into his arms and they kissed, softly at first, then with increasing passion. He stopped and stood back a bit, looking at her.

Scott said, "Give me a moment." Then she went to the kitchen and turned the oven off. She walked down the hallway toward the bedroom. She paused and looked back to see if he was following. He was still standing where she'd left him. She beckoned.

He removed his jacket and tie and laid them on the couch. As he started down the hallway toward the bedroom, he began removing his shirt. When he entered the bedroom, she was standing next to the bed, unbuttoning her blouse. He set his shirt on a chair and went to her.

"Let me."

***

Later, when they were still lying in bed touching and talking, she asked him about his day and whether he'd worked on his art. He said he had, but that he'd been a bit preoccupied by work and had gone in for a half day.

"So, tell me something," he asked, "These women that you counsel at the rape victims' clinic... you said you don't think any of them could kill the perp that attacked them. How sure are you?"

"Anything's possible, but I just don't think so. Most of them are not so much hostile as they are sad and confused."

"Confused?"

"Almost every one of them asks me the question: How could a good god let this happen to me?"

"So, what do you tell them?"

"Nothing. I listen. I help them work through things themselves."

Coxon raised himself on his elbow. "So what do you think? Why would a good god allow evil?"

"I figure I'm like a dog. A dog can understand some of what we say to it, but it can never speak our language. The answers to the big questions are as far beyond me as speaking English is to a dog."

She asked if he was hungry yet. When he nodded, she said she'd go and re-start dinner.

She went to the bathroom and closed the door. When she came out, she was dressed in a robe. "If you want to freshen up, there's a towel on the counter for you." She headed for the kitchen.

Coxon took a fast shower. When he finished toweling off, he opened the hamper to put the towel in. He saw something odd, stared at it trying to figure out what it was, then reached to pull it out. It was a black ski mask. He dropped it back in. He leaned his back against the wall with his eyes tightly shut. Now he knew what had been bugging him—a thought he didn't want to think.

When he had dressed, Coxon went to the living room, sipped his champagne, and carried her glass to her. As she worked on dinner, he walked around looking more closely at photos on the wall. He looked intently one of her in a Portland Police Department group shot.

"You were in the Portland Police Department? I thought you said Hillsboro, Oregon."

Scott set two plates on the table, along with a bottle of wine. "Hillsboro, where I lived, is a suburb of Portland."

They sat and they began to eat. She chatted about food and wine. He was silent, nodding occasionally. She couldn't figure out why he seemed so somber. "What are you thinking about?"

He stopped eating and sat back, finished his glass of champagne, and poured wine for both of them. "I'm thinking about work, and I guess I need to talk to you about it. See, a guy named Mark Mannon was castrated. We think it was done by the same perpetrator who mutilated and killed Pate." He went on to explain that Mannon had not been killed because the perpetrator had taken great care not to let him die.

When he'd finished telling her about Mannon, Scott said, "Interesting. Generically its the same crime, but with noteworthy differences. So, if this was an act of revenge, I guess Mannon's crime was lesser. What do you think?"

"I want *you* to tell *me*."

She thought he was asking her professional opinion, but there was something about the way he said it. He sounded edgy, almost aggressive. She said, "We should try to think like the avenger. He wants the punishment to be commensurate with the crime."

"Avenger. I like that. You said, 'he'. Does this avenger have to be a man?"

Scott was momentarily caught off guard. "I just assumed...well...I guess...well, it seems like a big task for a woman physically to overcome these men."

Coxon nodded and resumed eating. Casually he noted, "You know apparently Mannon was knocked unconscious with a well-placed blow."

She replied, "Anyone who understands karate well..." She caught herself and looked up to see him staring intently at her.

He answered, "That's what I was thinking. So, do you know any ninjas that might be avengers? Frankly you're the only ninja I know, but for the life of me, I cannot imagine your motive."

Offended, she said, "Chris, I certainly hope that you don't suspect me! I mean, just because I know karate and the second victim was chopped!" Her voice trailed off as she looked at him for reaction, trying to read him.

He looked at her with a mixture of sadness and resignation. She decided she would not lie to this man. "Why? What makes you think it could be me?"

"Just little things. Portland PD at the time of a similar mutilation. Volunteer at the Rape Crisis Center. Karate. Strongest woman I've ever known in more ways than one. Hamper."

Scott looked quizzical when he said the word *hamper*, then understanding dawned. She dropped her head into her hands. "Unbelievable. I must have been subconsciously trying to reveal it to you. A stunningly incompetent mistake."

"Anyway, the more I've gotten to know you, the more believable it is that you'd be capable of doing it. It's scary and I need to understand it. So, Sarah, just tell me. Tell me it isn't you."

She looked softly at him and sadly shook her head. She'd had relationships based on lies before. She'd already promised herself that she wouldn't let that happen with Coxon. But she'd had no idea that her conviction would be tested so soon and in this way. After a long pause she asked, "Are you coming after me?"

Coxon slowly shook his head and looked away. It was a wonder to him that he had been the happiest man alive an hour ago and was now totally miserable—both emotions triggered by this same woman. Then he raised his head and met Scott's eyes. "I have no real evidence that it was you. But everything in my training and my whole career says I should try to find some. Yet everything in my heart tells me not to."

She started to say something, then thought better of it. It was better to let him talk.

He continued, "You know, Kang keeps telling me that Pate and Mannon deserved what they got. I always felt so sure that he was wrong. Now I find myself thinking more and more like him. Now I..."

He sighed heavily and looked away. He took a sip of wine. Still, she waited silently.

"God, I am in a hell of a quandary, falling for someone I suspect of murder. I have some sorting out to do and I am not even sure where to begin. I just don't know what to do or even what to think."

"If it helps you any, I didn't plan on falling for a guy who could hunt me down—with the one guy who is probably clever enough to put me away."

"Like I said, there's a lot of thinking and sorting to be done. I have decided that I want to put us on hold. I'm just not sure of what I should do, or even what I can do. Things are pretty complicated for me. But I need to know something. Are you going to keep doing this?"

She'd been afraid of that question. She told him that she had intended to stop, but that she was reconsidering that decision because of the spree of the serial rapist murderer. If it could be proved to her satisfaction that the killer was George Lehman, and if he were not put away, then she might go after him.

He stood and paced, shaking his head in a mixture of anger and consternation. He put his hands on the back of his chair and leaned looking at her. "Sarah, you absolutely have to stop. There is a better way."

"I act only when the better way fails and I know for sure that it has."

"No, I mean a better way to get Lehman. We have to do this right. And I mean all of us, you, me, all of us. I want you to promise me that you will help me get him and you won't do your avenger thing."

She nodded. "Of course, I prefer doing it the right way. And of course, I will help however I can in that regard."

He paced around some more, again stopping to look at the Portland photo.

She said, "I have thought a lot about him and what he is likely to do next. This last incident gave him great confidence. He thinks he can beat you. He feels invincible. I also think he wants his own revenge against Cummins. My bet is he'll go for her as soon as he's well enough."

"Then that's how we'll catch him. Will you help me talk to Marilyn Cummins Monday morning? She is bait."

"Of course."

He explained that he was serious about placing their relationship on hold. So, he thought it best if he were to leave even before dinner was finished.

She ruefully smiled and said, "Aside from what we did together tonight, there is something else that I had envisioned for the evening, something I really wanted to do. Since I may not ever have the opportunity again, would it be alright if we have one dance before you go. I know it is an odd request, but I have wondered how you'd be and it would be...well, would you?"

He laughed, shook his head as if he couldn't quite believe it, and held out his hand to her. "Do you jitterbug?"

She stood and took his hand and, with the other, used a remote to turn on a player. It was Bonnie Raitt's *Shake A Little*.

He laughed and took her into his arms to dance. He thought, how could she know that he liked Bonnie Raitt?

When it was over, she said, "Just like I thought you'd dance."

He grinned, "You too."

Without another word he picked up his jacket and tie and headed for the door. She followed him. He turned and looked at her sadly. He kissed his finger, then touched her lip. He stepped out and closed the door.

***

He took a long walk toward the river. Had he been asked to imagine the craziest outcome imaginable for this night, he wouldn't have been able to predict such a wild set of events.

How could it be that he simultaneously felt such extremes. He was elated that he'd made love with the most interesting, beautiful creature he'd encountered in years, and that she'd even said she was falling for him. She excited and delighted him.

At the same time, he was shocked and horrified that she was a murderer, a vigilante who would mutilate and then kill. And, he wondered, what made her like that? How could she be so smart and competent, yet be so morally bankrupt that she could be the avenger?

He was quite sure that this was a seminal moment, a marker of time. Forever, for the rest of his life, events would henceforth be cataloged as either "before that Saturday night with Sarah" or "after that night."

***

You can be genuinely innocent, thought Marilyn Cummins, and still you can be mercilessly punished. And that is how she felt: punished without justification. She'd been harassed by a co-worker in the distant past until she'd finally lashed out. For that, she'd gone through hell. When finally she'd put it all behind her, got a new job, built a new life, it had all come back to wreck her again.

To her, the case was open and shut. The slimeball named Lehman had broken into her house and come to harm her. She'd shot in self-defense. Now, she was potentially going to be tried for having shot him. What should she have done, not shot him and let him hurt or even kill her? And why would they dredge up the irrelevant past and use it against her? Nothing was fair; nothing made sense to her.

It was Monday afternoon and Cummins was back in the conference room at the police station waiting for the detectives to come in and talk to her again. They'd had a discussion in late morning that had really upset her. They had taken a lunch break to give Cummins some time to herself.

In came Coxon, Kang, Scott, and two uniformed officers. After they all sat down, turned on the recorder, and Coxon asked, "Marilyn, did you think things over? Do you have any questions?"

Cummins was nervous, biting her nails and fidgeting. She spoke a bit too loudly, "Okay, so like, the plan is that I go nowhere without lett'n you know where I'm goin'. I get someone to go with me when I go out. And you want the wacko creep to come to my house again and try to hurt me again."

Coxon said, "That's putting it a bit harshly. We want to put communication equipment in your house so that if he comes, you will be able to call us immediately. And we want you to keep in close touch with us."

One of the uniformed officers explained how they'd have microphones in all her rooms by the next day and squad cars would drive by periodically all night.

Cummins was increasingly agitated, "What if he says nothin'? What if he comes in and kills me like instantly?"

"We'll be right there. He won't be able to."

"I want my gun back."

"That's not possible. We can't arm you."

Cummins began to cry. "You know, I really don't understand. If you like catch him attempting to rape or kill me...well, that won't be enough to put him away for very long, if at all. He'll get out and he'll just come after me again!"

Kang felt totally sympathetic, but had to say, "If we don't do this trap for him, he'll be out there waiting to attack you or someone else in the future. We have nothing to put him away with now. If we catch him trying to hurt you, we can at least get him locked up for a while."

"This is so stupid. You should be able to get the guy locked up forever!"

Scott gently placed her hands on Cummins'. "Marilyn, you're right, but there isn't a way to lock him up at all without your help. If it will make you feel better, I'll drive you home tonight and, starting tomorrow, either I or someone else will stay with you at night."

Coxon gave Scott a sharp look of disapproval.

Cummins quit crying and was relieved. "Yeah, like that would make me feel, you know, much safer."

Coxon said, "We can have an officer stationed in the house."

Cummins shook her head. "I'd prefer Dr. Scott."

They covered a few more details and wrapped it up. Scott and Cummins left together.

***

Coxon, scowling, left for the gym even though it was Monday and not a day he usually exercised. He was slamming his fists into a punching bag, sweating heavily.

Kang entered the gym and located him. He watched a moment and then approached. "Thought I'd find you here."

Coxon gave a few more punches, then stopped and put a towel around his head. He leaned his back against the wall, but said nothing.

Kang asked, "Got a moment for me? Or do you have more to do?"

"Nah. I'm done." He began walking toward the locker room with Kang following.

Coxon opened his locker and Kang sat on a nearby bench. No one else was around.

"I just came by to see if you want to talk. You nearly took off the head of anyone who got near you today. Then in the Cummins meeting... the icy formality between you and Dr. Scott was phenomenal."

"I told you. These cases are eating me alive."

"Well, maybe that's it. And maybe it's not. You and I have worked similar and tougher cases in the past. Never seen you lose your cool this way. Not even once. So that tells me something."

Coxon's temper flared, "So, what does it tell you, smart ass? If you know so damned much, who don't you just tell me about it?"

Kang lowered his voice by the same degree Coxon had raised his. "Okay, I will. It isn't about the case. It is about the girl."

Coxon slammed his locker door but said nothing. Kang waited a bit before saying, "So you are in love with her, but something isn't going right. She doesn't reciprocate? No, I doubt that's the problem. There's something more serious?

Coxon leaned his back against the lockers and crossed his arms. "I feel like I'm not the same person anymore. I'm not me. I always see the path ahead pretty clearly, but now I don't. I feel like I've lost my bearings."

"If you're in love, there's no point in fighting it. It takes over your soul. You don't have a choice."

"Amen to that."

"My advice is to treat it like a carnival ride. Enjoy the exhilaration to the fullest while it lasts."

Coxon growled with frustration. He threw his towel across the room.

Kang continued, "Okay. So, there's a more serious problem. But you don't want to talk about it and, of course, I respect that. But I hope you don't mind if I offer one more piece of advice?"

Coxon looked at him questioningly.

"Be your analytical self. Decide what you want the outcome to be, then identify the steps you have to take to get there. Otherwise, it'll keep eating you. There's a solution to whatever your problem is—maybe not an ideal one, but a solution. You just have to find it. Now, not later."

"As usual, partner, you're right. I've got to sort things out with her. And I'm sorry I've been a horse's ass today and I will get that under control. Tomorrow'll be better."

Kang nodded, stood, and turned for the door as Coxon walked toward the shower. Kang turned and called to Coxon, who stopped and turned.

"Chris, if you do love her, it is worth trying to get her to stop doing whatever it is that's bugging you. ...And, by the way, you remember what I said about wanting to find Pate's executioner out of curiousity? Well, I don't want to find that perpetrator now for any reason at all."

Then he waved and left.

***

Across town, Scott pulled into Cummins' driveway just after dark. They'd stopped to do a bit of grocery shopping. Cummins climbed out of the car with her bag and Scott was waiting to watch her get to the door and enter. But Cummins walked around to the driver's side. Scott rolled down the window.

"I'm really like nervous you know. You say the setup won't be ready until tomorrow. What if he, you know, comes tonight? What if he's like already in my house?"

"Marilyn, it's really too soon. His wound probably hasn't even healed. Also, he has historically waited weeks between strikes. It's been only a few days."

Cummins didn't budge.

Scott tried another tack. "You've been here every night alone since he attacked you. Why are you so much more afraid now?"

Cummins began to cry again. "It's obvious. You, the expert, have informed me that he's coming for me again! And I'm supposed to be like, like a lure!"

"Look, I'll go in first and check out the house. You stay here. Lock yourself in my car. Then we'll go in together. After I leave, you can lock up. I'll come back here at eleven PM and will spend the night. How's that?"

Cummins nodded and handed Scott the house keys. Scott got out and headed for the house. Cummins locked herself in the car.

Scott unlocked the door and stepped in, searching for the light. She turned it on and went room to room, making sure no one was there. She started up the stairs, stepping on a step that creaked loudly.

Scott entered the bedroom, flicked on the light, and walked toward the bathroom. From behind her, the closet door crashed open and Lehman jumped on her back. He tightened his forearm against her neck and began to strangle her. She reached her left leg behind his right leg and brought her arm around sharply, causing him to lose balance and fall over her leg backwards.

Lehman then saw Scott was not Cummins and was surprised enough to pause. She took advantage and kicked his wounded thigh. He screamed and lunged, catching her leg. She fell backward. They both scrambled to their feet. He ran forward and got both hands around her neck.

She brought her arm around and stabbed two fingers into his throat, but her reach was insufficient to inflict much pain. She brought her other arm over his head, twisting her body with the motion and thus breaking his grip on her throat. He threw a punch that knocked her backward into the wall. She knew she couldn't let him hit her again or she might go down.

Scott ran around the room, throwing objects in his path to give herself a moment to recover. Then, in an open area, she turned to confront him.

He drew out a knife and began to sidle toward her. She made a move to disarm him by hitting both sides of his wrist simultaneously, but she was too slow. He slashed at her and gashed her forearm deeply. Then he paused, took a step backward and threw the knife. She tried to dodge, but it penetrated her upper arm.

Scott ran at him, leapt into the air, and kicked his sternum hard. He went down. She kicked again, breaking his nose. He rolled into a fetal position. She kicked his kidney hard.

Lehman crawled away from her. He struggled to his knees and held up his palms as if to surrender. As he raised his head, she powered the outside edge of her flat hand into his adam's apple. He collapsed. She kicked him as hard as she could in the temple. She waited a minute while she wrapped her forearm, then checked to make sure he was no longer breathing.

She took out her cell and called 911.

***

Later that night, Scott was lying on a hospital bed with her arm and shoulder fully bandaged. Coxon was at her side.

"I hear you're okay, thank God. But you'll have some interesting scars to show everyone."

She smiled tiredly. He stood quietly for a few moments and then said, "Look I know it isn't the right time to talk about this, but I want you to know that as soon as you are well enough, we really need to talk. There is a lot I don't understand, and I've decided I want to."

Scott was a little weak from ordeal. Her voice was soft, almost distant. "Nothing to talk about. I got him."

"Yeah, I guess you did."

Scott put out her hand and grasped his tie, tugging him gently toward her. He leaned close.

"If there aren't any more, will you take us off of hold?

Coxon straightened and looked at her. He took her hand and kissed it.

"Most definitely."

ABOUT THE AUTHOR

Kathleen Cordelia Bailey (b. 1949) earned a PhD in political science from the University of Illinois after a year's research in 1973-74 in Tehran, Iran. Thereafter, she held several jobs in government service. Throughout her career, whatever she was doing to earn a living, Bailey maintained a strong interest in the arts. She is a painter, fine-art photographer, filmmaker, and author of fiction as well as non-fiction.

In 2003, she was watching a movie with her husband at home when a disturbing scene involving an attack against a woman made her leave the room. Upon return, she asked her husband why movies frequently showed women under attack, but rarely did they fight back successfully. Her husband replied that she should write her own movie. So, she did. She completed the script that year and entitled it *Revenge In Kind*. This novella is the story as based on the original version of the screenplay.

www.ingramcontent.com/pod-product-compliance
Lightning Source LLC
Chambersburg PA
CBHW060400130626
46556CB00013B/1842